SAVAGE PAGAN

A successful, beautiful model, Lisa could have had her pick of husbands. But instead she found herself forced to marry the haughty Rick Andreas, who apparently despised her as much as she disliked him. How had she managed to get herself into such a predicament?

SAVAGE PAGAN

BY

HELEN BIANCHIN

MILLS & BOON LIMITED
15–16 BROOK'S MEWS
LONDON W1A 1DR

First published 1984
Australian copyright 1984
Philippine copyright 1984
This edition 1984

© Helen Bianchin 1984

ISBN 0 263 74604 6

Set in 10 on 12 pt Linotron Times
05–0684–54,105

Photoset by Rowland Phototypesetting Ltd
Bury St Edmunds, Suffolk
Printed in Great Britain by
Richard Clay (The Chaucer Press) Ltd,
Bungay, Suffolk

CHAPTER ONE

Lisa cast a final hasty glance at her mirrored reflection, then moved out from the backstage dressing-room towards the curtain.

There was nothing to indicate that this afternoon's fashion show would be any different from countless others in which she had participated over the past few years. The taped orchestration on this occasion was cacophonous jazz, and to her slightly jaded ears it appeared to be reaching ear-splitting proportion.

Within seconds the music came to a sudden stop, and the organiser began an introductory speech, then the compère took over the microphone and began her professional spiel regarding the merits of the gown about to be modelled.

On cue, Lisa moved out on to the stage. Her expression bore a pensive, faintly aloof air, her fine brown eyes wide and clear as she went through the choreographical movements with graceful dignity. Keeping her gaze high, she skimmed the heads of the audience, noting with idle interest that the hall appeared filled to capacity. Then with skilled fluidity she took the catwalk—pausing, turning, smiling, before returning to the stage where she effected one last turn, then moved through the curtain to backstage.

'Did you see that gorgeous-looking man near the rear of the hall?'

Lisa paused long enough to give the owner of that

faintly breathless voice a slight frown, and shook her head in silent negation.

'Far left corner,' Susie murmured, rolling her eyes expressively. 'Tall, dark, in an impeccable business suit. Wow!' Then it was her turn to move through the curtain and take up where Lisa had left off.

Organised chaos reigned in the dressing-room, with barely room to move for the five models employed for the charity-raising function. The art of quick-change was something Lisa had acquired during the past three years, and now she slipped out of her dress and donned another with the ease of long practice, crossing to the mirror to smooth her hair and run a check on her make-up.

Five minutes later she took the catwalk again, and as she completed a turn at its end she let her eyes skim slowly to the left corner, more from curiosity than anything else. Accustomed to male admiration, and accomplished in dealing with it, she was unprepared for the dark probing gaze centred on her slim figure. His features appeared ruggedly stern and uncompromising, and she perceived that he was aggressively attractive rather than handsomely good-looking. World-weary and cynical, Lisa added silently as she made her way back to the stage, and she actually *felt* those dark eyes observe her every move, dissecting and categorising in ruthless evaluative criticism that brought a surge of angry resentment.

'Did you see him?' Susie whispered as Lisa entered the dressing-room. 'Isn't he the dishiest male you've seen in a long time?'

'He doesn't do a thing for me,' she murmured with deliberate uninterest. *Liar!* His image rose to taunt her, and with a gesture of irritation she peeled off her dress.

The next time she looked he was no longer there, and she unconsciously relaxed, completing the afternoon's assignment with professional ease.

It was almost five o'clock when she eased her car out from its parking space and headed it towards the city. Her apartment was situated in suburban Lane Cove on the other side of Sydney's harbour. Given some luck and possible celestial assistance she might make it home by six, then she had to shower and change in order to meet her brother and sister-in-law for dinner. She was in half a mind to cancel, pleading a long day and a headache, but James had been insistent when he'd phoned that morning—almost adamant, and she was immensely fond of him.

The traffic was predictably heavy, moving at times with a snail-like pace as it poured through the city streets on to various freeways, but once over the Harbour bridge Lisa made progress.

The apartment was just as she'd left it early that morning, and she crossed into the kitchen to make a much-needed cup of coffee, then moved to the lounge and switched on the electric fire.

Tossing her coat on to a nearby chair, she eased off her shoes and sank down onto the sofa. Any minute now the phone would ring and Tony would expect a recount of her day. A slight smile tugged the edge of her lips. Dear uncomplicated Tony! He really cared about her, more *friend* than boy-friend, although she was aware he didn't regard her in a similar light. Of late, he'd been pushing to deepen the relationship, and couldn't understand the reason for her hesitation.

Almost on cue, the kettle whistle blew, and she had just switched it off and poured water into the cup when the phone pealed an insistent summons.

'Hi there,' she answered warmly, and heard his chuckle in response.

'How was your day?'

'Busy. A gruelling session at the studio, followed by a fashion show this afternoon. I've just got in.' She took a sip of hot coffee and felt its reviving effect.

'Care to meet for a few drinks?'

'Oh, Tony—I can't,' she refused. 'Not tonight.'

'You haven't succumbed to one of your lecherous admirers, have you?' he hazarded jokingly, and she teased lightly,

'Five at least. There's safety in numbers.'

'Surely you jest—I hope.'

Sensing his need for reassurance, Lisa unhesitatingly gave it. 'I'm dining out with James and Ingrid.'

'Alone?'

A slight frown creased her brow. 'I'm not sure. James didn't say.'

'How about tomorrow night? Dinner, perhaps?'

'Fine,' she agreed. 'Pick me up at seven. Now I have to dash. 'Bye!' Replacing the receiver, she finished her coffee, then crossed into the bedroom.

She wished there was time for a leisurely bath, but she'd have to make do with a quick shower instead. As to what she would wear—a mental image of her wardrobe's contents flashed through her brain, and she unerringly made a selection, her mind's eye settling on its accessories before she stepped into the shower stall.

Some fifteen minutes later Lisa put the finishing touches to her make-up, then stood back from the mirror and carefully scrutinised her reflected image.

She bore an air of classic elegance, attired in a figure-hugging dress of lightweight cream wool with a silken scarf knotted carelessly about her neck. Her skin was flawless, and the skilful use of shadow, eyeliner and mascara highlighted startingly eloquent brown eyes which were by far her best feature, she accorded silently as she viewed their mirrored depths from beneath long, dark-fringed lashes.

With a faint sigh she turned away from the dressing table and caught up a fur-trimmed suede coat from the bed, slipped her arms into the sleeves, then she moved towards the front door.

In the hallway she summoned the elevator and waited patiently for its arrival, her expression becoming faintly pensive as it transported her down to the underground car park.

The invitation to join James and his wife for dinner was vaguely perplexing, especially as she had spent the previous evening in their company. Older by some eleven years, her brother had taken her beneath his protective wing more than five years ago when their parents had been tragically killed in a small plane crash. Even now, despite her twenty-two years, he still regarded her as his 'little' sister, and tended to treat her in much the same manner as he did his two children.

His disapproval had been voluble when she had elected to embark on a modelling career at seventeen, but as time progressed and she achieved recognition, she had succeeded in earning his reluctant admiration. There was something immensely pleasing in having her photograph in a variety of fashion magazines, the knowledge that she possessed the necessary *élan* to show designer clothes to their best advantage. Yet there was no conceit in her manner—if anything, she strived not to let her acclaim to fame make any difference to friendships she had formed. Apart from a few, most men wanted to date her merely for the glamour they thought her presence might afford them, and the women were frankly and often nastily envious. It was useless to reveal how desperately hard she had had to work those first few years, explain that hours posing beneath hot lights in a photographic studio was anything but fun. Fashion modelling possessed an aura of glamour, and most were ignorant of the gruelling work it involved. Yet there were times when she became tired of always being on display, intensely vulnerable to criticism.

On the surface she had everything a girl could want. A luxurious apartment in one of Sydney's fashionable North Shore suburbs; she drove a sports coupé, and owned innumerable clothes whose designer labels were the envy of many. Even marriage could be hers, if she chose to give Tony the slightest encouragement. Yet she hesitated, stalling each time he broached the subject, unwilling to make a final commitment. She liked him, felt comfortable in his presence, but some inner voice kept taunting that there had to be more to a relationship than mere compatibility. His kisses didn't transport her anywhere, and never had she been tempted to defy moral convention. Sometimes she wondered if she shouldn't simply give in and sleep with him—if only to bury the bogey of her own virginity.

Lisa unlocked the door of her metallic silver Mazda RX7 and slid in behind the wheel, experiencing a feeling of satisfaction when the engine sprang to life. Carefully she eased the car out from its parking space, then sent it purring towards the ramp leading out on to the street.

The drive to Clontarf took almost twenty minutes,

and her sister-in-law let her into the imposing brick house with a finger against her lips in cautionary silence.

'Simon and Melissa are on the verge of sleep,' Ingrid murmured. 'If they hear your voice, they'll be down-stairs in a flash demanding instant attention!' She ushered Lisa in with one hand and closed the door behind her with the other. 'James particularly wants to get away on schedule,' she explained with a slight smile. 'Time being of the essense, you understand.'

Lisa wrinkled her nose, and her fine brown eyes sparkled with wicked humour. 'You're beginning to sound like my dear brother! He should have chosen to enter the legal fraternity—as a judicial personage, he'd have been perfect,' she concluded quizzically.

'Missed my vocation, have I?' a droll voice teased from behind, and Lisa swung round with a smile.

'Hi, big brother,' she proffered teasingly. 'Your use of the normal phrase tends towards unctuous civility—fine in the boardroom, but a trifle overwhelming for lesser mortals. How are you?'

His response was immediate. 'Fine. So pleased you could join us this evening.'

'I'll fetch my coat,' Ingrid excused, moving from the lounge.

'I'm not sure I'd have dared not to,' Lisa grinned. 'You were rather adamant when you rang this morning.'

'Sorry about the short notice.'

'So you should be,' she rebuked teasingly. 'I had other arrangements far more pressing than being taken out to dinner.'

'I'm sorry. However—'

'Oh, really, James,' she laughed, 'I'm not being serious!'

He viewed her solemnly, and there was no answering twinkle in his eyes. 'It's very important you accompany us.'

'Good heavens!' she exclaimed, her eyebrows winging high in mock astonishment. 'Who's joining us? Some exalted Member of Parliament you particularly want to impress?'

He seemed on the point of imparting information, then appeared to change his mind. 'A man whose status and power command immense respect,' he revealed slowly, and she swept him a quick glance.

'You sound almost—apprehensive.'

'Rick Andreas isn't someone you can easily ignore,' James declared heavily.

'Am I to be there as a diversionary tactic?' Lisa quizzed lightly, and glimpsed his faint frown.

'Not at all,' he reproved. 'Socially, you're very much an asset.'

'I see,' she mused. 'I'm merely an inclusion to even up numbers between the sexes. Is that it?'

James appeared to have trouble assembling the correct words, and he began ponderously, 'Actually, I'd take it as a personal favour if you could—er—' he paused, then continued delicately—'be—nice to him.'

This was becoming more curious by the minute! 'Precisely how *nice*?' she questioned, and he gave a slight shrug of impatience.

'Indulge in sophisticated small-talk,' he elaborated. 'You know the sort of thing.'

'Captivate him with my fine wit and intelligence,' she essayed with a grin. 'Is that it?' A faint grimace tugged the edge of her mouth. 'Just as long as I'm not expected to play the *femme fatale*.'

'Really, Lisa,' James reproved, 'there's no need to be facetious.'

At that precise moment Ingrid returned, coat in hand, and James took it from her, holding it out so that she could slip her arms into its sleeves.

'The children are asleep, bless their sweet hearts,' Ingrid told him. 'The babysitter has been briefed. Shall we go?'

Seated in the rear of her brother's car, Lisa stifled a tiny smile. Like its owner, the Volvo sedan was the epitome of functional stability. It had style and elegance, but lacked the flair of its racier counterparts. Take her RX7, or a Porsche . . . But therein lay the difference. James was strictly conventional, even *staid*. While she had a capacity for fun, a wicked sense of humour on occasion that had more than once led her into strife with the strict nuns who had been in charge of her convent education.

The restaurant was an exclusive establishment located in the prestigous suburb of Potts Point.

'My, my,' Lisa murmured as James led them inside. 'If you want to impress, this is the place to do it.'

'Precisely. I suggested we meet at the bar, although we're a little ahead of time.'

'That's my brother—never late,' she accorded with an indistinct grin. She stood silently as the elegantly attired *maître d'hôtel* came forward and checked their booking, then she moved in Ingrid's wake as they were ushered to the bar. 'Is this to be a cosy foursome, or will there be others joining us?'

'A whisky and soda, brandy, lime and lemonade, and—Lisa, what will you have?'

'I'll join Ingrid. James, do answer the question,' she

pursued. 'I don't like it when you're evasive.'

'Louise and Peter Beresford,' he informed her, his gaze moving towards the main entrance. 'They've just come in.'

'Hooray,' Lisa declared beneath her breath. This was going to be a fun evening. Peter Beresford was one of her brother's associates, and punctilious. His wife was intensely shy and needed constant cajoling to enter into any conversation.

The pleasantries dispensed with, Lisa sipped the contents of her glass, enjoying the relaxing effect the brandy was having. She was hungry, the result of a hurried snack shortly before midday, and little time in which to eat thereafter. A photographic assignment that morning in Sacha's studio had been trying—and cold, despite the slight warmth generated from the arc lighting. Beachwear, especially minuscule bikinis, could hardly be classed as adequate clothing in a southern hemispheric winter.

Ingrid and Louise appeared totally engrossed in recounting the exploits of their respective offspring, while James and Peter were arguing the merits of various stocks and bonds. Feeling slightly *passé*, Lisa twirled the remaining contents of her glass and pondered when the guest of honour would deign to put in an appearance.

'Ah, here's Andreas now.'

Some sixth sense warned of an impending premonition, and all her fine body hairs rose in defence as she *felt* his presence an instant before he entered her peripheral vision.

James effected the necessary introductions with ease, concluding, 'My sister, Lisa—Rick Andreas.'

Lisa felt her eyes widen with shock as she encountered

the broad frame of the man standing before her. The compelling stranger who had viewed part of this afternoon's fashion show and her brother's business acquaintance were one and the same! At a distance he had looked infinitely dynamic, but up close she detected an elemental ruthlessness that was vaguely disquieting. Dangerous, she amended, viewing his magnetically arresting features with polite uninterest.

'How do you do,' she greeted formally, proffering him the slightest of smiles, and her eyes widened fractionally as his dark mocking eyes embarked on a leisurely appraisal of each and every one of her visible attributes before returning to meet her startled gaze.

'Good evening.' His voice was a deep, slightly accented drawl, and he moved to take the empty seat between Ingrid and herself.

She felt suddenly breathless, aware of her erratic pulsebeat as she surreptitiously watched him order a drink, then lift the glass to his lips. An instinctive nagging doubt rose unbidden to her mind, demanding verification, and she spared her brother a swift glance, incurring his expansive smile with an equanimity she was far from feeling. James, in the role of matchmaker? He knew better, surely!

'I imagine we should be honoured you've elected to join us this evening, Mr Andreas,' Lisa remarked with distant civility, and glimpsed his cynical amusement.

'Not at all,' he slanted dryly. 'It's an occasion I couldn't be tempted to miss.'

'Good heavens!' She deliberately feigned surprise. 'I can't think why.'

His dark eyes were startlingly direct. 'What man would

pass up an opportunity to have dinner with a beautiful woman?'

Her lips curved into a slow smile. 'Am I supposed to be flattered?'

'Are you?'

Her lashes swept upwards with apparent lack of guile. 'Did you mean me to be?'

'Perhaps you should tell me about yourself,' Rick Andreas drawled sardonically, and she uttered a tinkling laugh.

'Really, Mr Andreas,' she mocked lightly, 'you can't really want to know.'

'Rick,' he insisted softly, his gaze probing and faintly analytical, until she felt compelled to glance away.

No man had ever ruffled her composure to such an extent. It seemed as if some master switch had been pulled deep inside her, generating a multitude of latent sensations that sent every nerve-end pulsing into awareness.

'Perhaps we could trade life histories, and make it last all the way through dinner,' she suggested with unaccustomed flippancy. 'Although I'll wager your background is far more colourful than mine.'

'You think so?'

'I'm sure the life I lead must be deadly dull in comparison,' she suggested dryly.

'Aren't you being presumptuous?'

She met his gaze and held it. 'I'm at a loss to know why you're here. This couldn't be termed a business dinner, so it can only be assumed to be a social occasion.' A polite dismissive smile etched her generous mouth. 'If, as I suspect, you've inveigled the invitation, I should warn that blind dates have never been my thing.'

His eyes darkened with something she failed to define. 'What is your "thing", Lisa Gray?'

The softly voiced query startled her, sending a frisson of apprehension slithering down her spine. She had started out in control, playing a cat and mouse game, and suddenly she found her role had been reversed.

Perhaps it was as well that the *maître d'hôtel* summoned them to their table, and on being handed a menu she pretended to study it, giving the extensive list of courses her entire attention.

Ingrid and James, together with Louise and Peter, were *there*, but the only person she was totally aware of was the hatefully cynical man seated mere inches to her left.

'May I offer a suggestion?'

His drawling voice brought all her hackles to the fore, and every nerve and fibre screamed out for the evening to be over and done with.

'I'm quite capable of making a selection.'

One eyebrow rose in sardonic query. 'Did I imply that you were not?'

Slanting him a sweet smile, she ordered a starter, and followed it with a salad. 'May I have a Perrier?' She daren't have any more alcohol. As it was, the two brandies were beginning to have a dulling effect, and she needed all her faculties alert if she was to keep pace with the inestimable Rick Andreas.

'You are a model.'

Lisa replaced the fork on to her entrée dish and waited until it had been removed before answering. 'Do you disapprove?'

His slow gleaming smile did strange things to her equilibrium. 'I don't imagine it would matter if I did.'

'Oh, I see,' she answered obliquely. 'You needn't feel obliged to indulge in polite conversation.'

'On the contrary,' he drawled, 'I'm fascinated.' His dark eyes flared with cynical mockery, and she stilled the silent rage that threatened to rise to the surface.

'Really?' She deliberately held his gaze. 'There's more to it than merely being a clothes-horse, as most people imagine it entails. Photographic modelling means working one season ahead—swimwear in winter, fur coats in summer.' Her nose wrinkled in vivid recollection of the morning's session. 'Fashion parades that involve split-second timing, and being adept at the art of quick-change. Matching the mood to the clothes. Being available to drive or fly to an off-beat location.' Her chin lifted fractionally at his indolent interest. 'The competition is fierce, and the lifestyle purported to be far more glamorous than it actually is.'

'You make it sound like hard work.'

He was amused, darn him! 'Believe me, for the most part it is.' Her lips tightened fractionally, then relaxed into a seeming smile. 'Your turn, Mr Andreas.'

'Rick,' he corrected with dangerous softness. 'I insist.'

'I doubt we'll see each other again after this evening,' she declared evenly, and glimpsed the cynical gleam evident in his dark eyes.

'What makes you think that?'

An involuntary shiver slithered its way down to the base of her spine. She didn't want to see him again, and especially not alone. Some strange chemistry had to be responsible for the way her body was reacting, resulting in a heightened awareness that seemed too complex for her to assimilate. Rick Andreas was the antithesis of everything she admired in a man. To *date* him would be akin to juggling a jar of nitro-glycerine! Aloud she ventured, 'Are you one of James' business associates?'

One eyebrow slanted in musing mockery. 'Question and answer time?'

'Why not?' Lisa demanded coolly. 'Fair's fair, after all.'

His eyes held sardonic amusement, and she watched as he lifted his glass and took a generous swallow, noting the lean strength of his hand and the strong set of his jaw.

'I head a consortium involved in finance and property management,' he informed her silkily, and she stifled a wry grimace.

'Something which covers a broad spectrum, I imagine.'

His smile was totally without humour. 'Indeed?'

'What else is left?' Lisa hazarded with sarcasm. 'The weather?'

'You could dance with me,' he slanted, his expression assuming cynical amusement as she shook her head. 'Afraid, Lisa?' he taunted softly, and she shot him a quelling glance.

'Not in the least.' Brave words! It was bad enough having to sit within such close proximity, without being held in his arms.

'I find that difficult to believe.'

Oh, he was impossible! 'If you're trying to goad me into accepting, you're wasting your time,' she said coldly.

'Are you usually this defensive with your boy-friend?'

Her eyebrows rose in an expression of mockery. 'What makes you think I have one?'

Amusement tugged the edges of his sensuously-moulded mouth. 'It would be extremely hard to believe a girl with your attributes is without a male-companion, shall we say?'

Resentment lent a fiery sparkle to her eyes. 'What difference does it make whether I have one—or *several*, for that matter?' she snapped. 'It's none of your business.'

His silence was enervating, and it was a relief when the waiter arrived with their main course. Lisa deliberately sought conversation with Ingrid and Louise, enticing both women into discussing the merits of a play she knew they had seen the previous week.

Such a time-consuming topic lasted until coffee was served, and her defection didn't seem to bother Rick Andreas at all, although once when she chanced a glance in his direction she was disconcerted to meet the musing cynicism evident and knew he wasn't in the least fooled!

It was almost eleven when they vacated the restaurant, and Lisa gave an inaudible sigh of relief when no one suggested they move on to take in a show. She had an early assignment the next morning, and Roberto would only cluck like a mother hen if she arrived with shadows beneath her eyes.

'Goodnight, Lisa.'

She turned and met Rick Andreas' faintly mocking gaze, and gave him a slight smile. 'Goodbye, Mr Andreas,' she corrected with soft emphasis. 'So nice to have met you.' The last was tritely uttered, and bore no resemblance to the words conveyed. She caught a flash of white teeth, then he took his leave and moved with pantherish grace towards the car park.

Seated comfortably in the rear of James' Volvo she endeavoured not to give the evening too much thought—Rick Andreas least of all!

'What did you think of our fellow guest?' James turned the car into the steady stream of traffic and accelerated until they were travelling at a reasonable speed. His query was carefully noncommittal, and Lisa drew a deep calming breath.

'What do you want me to say?' she parried lightly, catching sight of his studious profile in the rear-vision mirror. A faint frown worried her brow, and she was unable to prevent the feeling that there was more to the evening's invitation than met the eye.

'An—uncomfortable man,' Ingrid offered, taking the query generally. 'Oh, he was extremely polite, darling,' she hurried on, catching her husband's penetrating glance. 'His manner is vaguely—menacing. Almost savagely elemental,' she concluded slowly.

'Good heavens, Ingrid!' James discounted in outrage. 'You've been reading too many romantic novels!'

'Perhaps it's because he's foreign, darling,' his wife soothed. 'Andreas is a name of Greek origin, surely? And he does speak with just the slightest accent.'

'He's brilliant in his field,' he muttered, refusing to be placated. 'Quite without equal.'

'I'm sure he is,' Ingrid attempted to appease. 'I was merely commenting from a personal viewpoint, not referring to his business acumen.'

'Why did he join us tonight?' Lisa enquired without any real interest. 'It could hardly be described as a business dinner.'

James appeared to pause, then his shoulders moved in to form a light shrug. 'He professed an interest to meet you.'

Now it was her turn to be surprised. 'For heaven's sake—why?'

'Don't be naïve, Lisa,' he dismissed ponderously. 'You're a very attractive young woman.'

'Do you mean to tell me this evening was organised expressly for that purpose?' she demanded, feeling unaccountably angry.

'I arranged an introduction,' James rationalised. 'Is that so terrible?'

'You could at least have been honest about it,' she threw heavily.

'You'd have refused,' he stated flatly, and she retaliated swiftly,

'You're darn right!'

'Oh, stop it, both of you,' Ingrid intervened. 'It was a pleasant evening, and there's no harm been done.'

'If we both survive to senility, I'll still be his *little* sister, and merit his so-called protection,' Lisa commented dryly. 'Unfortunately, this time I'm not amused.'

James was silent as he eased the Volvo into the driveway, and when the car came to a halt, she slipped out and crossed to where her Mazda was parked.

'I won't come in,' she declined, unlocking the door, then turning she bade them both goodnight. 'I'll call in at the weekend.'

She slid in behind the wheel, switched on the ignition, then with a carefree wave she sent the vehicle purring down the driveway.

CHAPTER TWO

THE insistent peal of the telephone caught Lisa un-
awares. Setting down her glass of freshly-squeezed
orange juice, she crossed the kitchen and lifted the
receiver, to hear James' voice on the line.

'Care to meet me for lunch?'

'I've a gruelling photographic session all morning, and
a fashion showing for a charity organisation this afternoon,' she told him a trifle ruefully. 'You've chosen a
bad day. Would tomorrow do instead?'

There was a slight pause, then he ventured, 'Can
you spare forty, perhaps fifty minutes? I can book a
table at Papillon, which is only half a block from the
studio. Give me a time, so that I can get there early
and order.'

Lisa did a swift mental calculation, then hazarded,
'One o'clock? I'll have a seafood starter, a small steak
and a side salad. No wine.'

'Fine,' James declared briskly. 'See you there.'

A tiny frown creased her brow as she replaced the
receiver. It was unusual for James to want to see her
alone. A quick glance at her watch determined she
didn't have time to contemplate any further. She had
half an hour in which to shower, change, and tidy up
before she had to leave for the city.

Her apartment was one of a block of twelve, and she
had furnished it to her taste, employing subtle neutral
shades with the carpet and furnishings as a background

for exotic prints. Bright-coloured cushions provided a startling contrast that was a visual delight.

Lisa took the elevator to the basement, then crossed to her allotted car space and unlocked the Mazda. Sacha's studio was located in the heart of the city, and after ten minutes spent fruitlessly searching for a space to park she resignedly joined the queue of motorists flowing into a municipal car-park.

'You're late,' Sacha declared without preamble as she entered the studio, and she tossed him a solemn smile.

'It's a few minutes before nine,' she stated equably. 'I'm early. Where's Roberto?'

'Here, darling.' A man in his mid-forties slipped into the room and crossed to place a customary peck on her cheek. 'Millie is waiting in the changing-room with the clothes. She knows their order.' His smile was paternal. 'Be a good girl and go and change. Then we can get this session on the road.'

They did, but not without a few flare-ups from Sacha, who, with predictable regularity, lapsed into his native French when she failed to deliver precisely the expression, the exact movement to complete his visual concept of what he wanted on celluloid. His work was without fault, and as a fashion photographer and choreographer, he was without equal. He demanded the impossible, and swore when his models didn't adhere to his instructions—insisting that if they were the best, as they were purported to be, they would possess some form of telepathic instinct as to what he wanted to project.

Working with him for more than an hour tended to be an annihilating experience, and more than one girl had been known to rush from the studio in tears, vowing never to return.

Having worked with him for nearly three years, Lisa had never given him the satisfaction of resorting to emotionalism, and had thereby earned his grudging respect. Not that anyone would know, judging from the cynical insults he threw at frequent intervals.

'That's it,' Sacha declared, rising up from his haunches, and with fluid grace he crossed the room and doused the arc lighting.

Lisa rose from the stool on which she had been precariously perched for the past ten minutes and lifted her arms above her head in an attempt to ease stiffened muscles. Thank heavens that was over!

'You were good,' Roberto commented appreciably. 'Our client won't have any complaints with this layout.'

'Do any of them *dare* complain?' she murmured, and glimpsed his humorous smile.

'Not often. Have lunch with me? We've an hour before the fashion show.'

She shook her head with genuine regret. 'I can't. I'm meeting my brother in—' she spared her watch a glance, 'five minutes. I've just time to change. But thanks, anyway,' she said kindly.

Lisa walked to the Papillon restaurant, entering its revered foyer with swift lithe steps, a smile on her lips as she was recognised, and she greeted James with affectionate enthusiasm as she took the seat held out for her.

'This is an unexpected pleasure.'

'Yes—well, we don't have much time alone together,' he murmured, looking vaguely ill at ease. 'I've ordered you a Perrier. You stipulated no wine.'

'Thanks.' She cast a ravenous glance at the food reposing before her. 'This will go down well. Shall we start?'

It was part-way through the starter that James cleared his throat and began half-heartedly, 'I imagine you've guessed the reason I want to speak to you alone is both private and confidential?'

Lisa lifted her head and tried to gather some clue from his expression. 'Is it something to do with Ingrid?' she hazarded gently, and incurred his slight frown.

'Ingrid? What makes you think that?'

She breathed a mental sigh of relief. 'You'd better get straight to the point. Otherwise I'll never learn just what this clandestine luncheon is all about,' she teased gently.

'I—' he paused, struggling to find the right words, then continued as if reciting well-learnt lines. 'I'm on the brink of financial disaster,' he plunged without pre-amble. 'The business will collapse unless I agree to a takeover by one of the large consortiums.'

The shock of his announcement was visible on her features, and she endeavoured to remain calm as she searched his worried face, glimpsing the utter dejection and despair evident.

'There is a possibility of an amalgamation,' James recounted slowly. 'A parent consortium will lend its name to ours, injecting essential funds, and trade will continue as a joint venture. I can retain a seat on the directorial board.' He took a deep steadying breath, then sipped his wine. 'The alternative is a direct sell-out of plant and equipment, termination of all existing employment—with barely sufficient funds to settle half the creditors.'

'You want my advice?' The thought seemed incredible.

He appeared to be fighting an inner battle, and it was

several seconds before he spoke. 'I consider there is only one course—amalgamation.'

'I'll go along with that. The firm has been solely "family" for more than two generations. No cost must be spared to retain the family logo, if only in part,' Lisa declared earnestly, and saw his gleam of approval.

'Father would have been proud of you.'

'For sanctioning what must be an obvious decision?' she queried, and James shook his head.

'There's more.'

'Like—what? Conditions?' she prompted. 'I know my position as one of the directors is merely a legal technicality, but if there's anything I should be aware of, I'd prefer to hear it from you.'

'It has been suggested that the proposed amalgamation be—er—sealed privately, as well as professionally,' he laboured on ponderously, and she cast him a startled glance.

'What on earth do you mean?'

'Cement the linking chain.'

'You're talking in riddles. Elaborate, James.' A strange sinking sensation began in the pit of her stomach, almost as if some elusive premonition was forcing recognition.

'Marriage,' he revealed slowly.

Never before had one single word had such an impact. 'I'm expected to *marry* some stranger simply to consolidate a business deal? You can't be serious!' The latter wasn't even a query, just a denying statement of fact.

'During the past few days I've done everything in my power to try to convince him otherwise,' her brother declared heavily. 'But nothing will sway him.'

'And if I don't—comply,' she began hardily, 'doubt-less he'll withdraw, and the deal won't go through.'

'I'm afraid so.'

Lisa replaced her knife and fork, and pushed the half-empty plate to one side. All of a sudden her appetite had gone. 'What sort of man would stipulate such a condition?' she demanded angrily, and caught James' wry grimace.

'A very shrewd businessman,' he accorded dryly, and her rage boiled over.

'Who, having seen my face in several fashion maga-zines, has decided to insist I be part of the deal.' The oath she released wasn't in the least ladylike, and she made no attempt to apologise. 'If I was an unattractive, insignificant little nobody, the situation wouldn't arise.'

James shifted uncomfortably in his chair. 'I shan't attempt to influence you.'

'My God!' she breathed with pious disregard. 'How can you expect me to believe that?'

His gaze was startlingly level. 'I've stated facts—untenable though they may be. If there was any other way out of this mess, believe me, I've thought of little else over the past few weeks in an effort to reach a solution.'

Lisa cast him a riveting glance. 'Presumably,' she began with unaccustomed viciousness, 'you'll indulge me the opportunity to meet this—' she hesitated frac-tionally—'hedonistic *pagan*, before committing myself?' A humourless laugh escaped her lips. 'Doubtless he's totally repugnant,' she declared. 'Fifty at least; short, balding and sporting a paunch.' A vivid mental picture made her shiver with distaste, and she lifted indignant eyes to direct him a strangely hurt look. 'How can you even contemplate suggesting I tie myself to such a man?'

James expelled a heavy sigh. 'If he resembled anything like you suggest, I would never have given it any consideration,' he defended. 'Believe me, Lisa, the man is the antithesis of a middle-aged debauchee.'

'Even if he resembled a Greek god, it still doesn't excuse him for insisting I take part in a form of human bondage!'

He cleared his throat, then proffered awkwardly, 'We dined with him last evening.'

Lisa's eyes closed momentarily in a gesture of self-defence. *Rick Andreas!* Even to *contemplate* such a liaison was madness. Marriage to such a man would be like throwing a Christian to the lions—with no doubt as to who was the sacrificial offering!

'You're asking a hell of a lot,' she said slowly, and heard his long-drawn-out sigh.

'There would be certain—advantages,' he attempted reasonably.

'I'm expected to toss Tony to one side, with little or no explanation, and marry this—this *barbarian*, thus ensuring the firm's survival. How *noble*!' she concluded hollowly.

'Marriage is a comfortable institution—necessary, if one wants to continue one's lineage.'

She looked at him with new eyes, trying to strip away the civilised veneer. 'Are you trying to tell me that you married Ingrid for other than love?'

James toyed with his partly-filled glass. 'I have the greatest admiration for her,' he defended, shooting her a brooding glare. 'Dammit, she's the mother of my children. I respect her enormously.'

'Poor James,' Lisa declared sadly. 'No consuming

fires of passion burn inside your manly breast—or heat your loins.'

'Lisa!' It was plain that he was shocked.

'Oh, hell,' she muttered inelegantly. 'I'm no longer *sixteen*!'

'That's no excuse to speak in such a—common manner!'

'Do you consider the sexual act to be common? I always imagined it to be a physical expression of love. Perhaps I've been deluding myself, and should substitute love for *lust*.'

'Marriage provides security,' he struggled on valiantly. 'If you marry Rick Andreas, you'll never have to worry about where the next dollar is coming from for the rest of your life.' He frowned at her, looking very much like a prevailing judge. 'In this day and age, that's not to be lightly dismissed.'

Her gaze was startlingly direct. 'What if I refuse?'

'The firm goes into receivership,' James declared bluntly. 'I face certain bankruptcy. Life, as Ingrid and the children have known it, will be a thing of the past.'

'You paint a very grim picture. In fact, I'm not sure I could live with myself, knowing it's in my power to avert such a tragedy.'

He appeared to be vying with his conscience. 'Would it be so bad?'

'How much time do I have to think about it?' Lisa asked pensively, and he gave a humourless laugh.

'Until five o'clock this afternoon.'

Now she did erupt, and her fury brought a fiery sparkle to her dark brown eyes, a tinge of pink to her smooth cheeks that only seemed to enhance her natural beauty. Standing to her feet, she gathered up her bag and slung its strap over her shoulder. 'You can tell Rick Andreas to go to *hell!*' she declared vehemently, then, immune to James' obvious embarrassment, she turned and walked from the restaurant without so much as a word of farewell.

In her car she went through the motions automatically, and it said much for her guardian angel that she reached the exclusive suburb of Vaucluse without incident.

Roberto was already in attendance, and as she entered the hall he paused in his conversation with the compère to accord her a smile.

Lisa returned it perfunctorily, then made her way backstage to the dressing-room where Millie was busily engaged in setting out a large variety of clothes, checking items off on her list, a customary frown of concentration creasing her brow.

With utter professionalism Lisa crossed to a nearby table and picked up the list, ran her finger down the items she was to model, then setting down her bag she extracted a silk wrap. Within minutes she had stripped to bra and panties, and after knotting the silk ties about her waist she crossed to the mirror and began attending to her make-up.

Susie and Leanne, two fellow models who were to participate in the show, appeared simultaneously, closely followed by Greg, and within minutes Roberto added his presence to give last-minute instructions.

The compère's voice began an introductory spiel announcing the creation Lisa was to model, and with an audible groan she caught up a belt from the nearby rack, secured it, then summoning a bright smile she moved out on to the stage, executed a few elegant movements and stepped towards the catwalk. It was at this moment she forgot the audience, concentrating on displaying the clothes she was wearing to their best possible advantage. For the most part she enjoyed what she did, and the only garments which caused her some discomfit were skimpy bikinis—some, little more than thin strips of silk that were a mere compromise against total nudity.

At last they reached the final section, swimwear, and Lisa was glad her assignment was a maillot. In vivid yellow-gold, it hugged her body like a second skin, showing her solarium-gained tan to enviable advantage. Her long sable-brown hair flowed unbound down her back, and it swung and moved like liquid silk with every step she took. With utter professionalism she undid the ties of the matching silk wrap-around skirt and slipped it off, hooking it over one shoulder as she swirled gracefully at the end of the catwalk before moving back towards the stage.

Quite what made her glance sideways at that precise moment she couldn't explain. It seemed as if her eyes were drawn by some elemental magnetism to those of a man standing indolently at ease at the rear of the seated audience. His rugged features were assembled into an enigmatic mask, and she could almost feel his gaze as it raked her slim form.

Damn him, she cursed mentally. What was *he* doing here? For an infinitesimal second she frowned, then, conscious of where she was, what she was doing, she summoned a brilliant smile, and with sparkling eyes she effected one last swirling turn, then to a burst of loud applause she waved a hand and disappeared behind the curtain.

'Phew!' she breathed with relief, and casting a deprecatory grin towards Leanne and Susie, murmured, 'I'm glad that's over!' She reached for her wrap, pushed her arms into it, then pulling the edges together thrust her hands into the capacious pockets. 'It's cold. Any chance of a hot cup of coffee when we've changed?'

'I believe it's all been arranged,' Greg told her, moving to her side. He reached out and put his hands on her shoulders, kneading the tense muscles there with considerable skill. 'You're all strung up,' he frowned, and she gave a slight shrug.

'I had a stiff session with Sacha this morning. Nothing seemed to please him.'

'He's the best there is,' he soothed. 'Why else would Roberto use him?'

'I'd better go and change,' Lisa decided as she moved her head in a slow circle, then reversed the motion. 'I don't suppose you could find me some aspirin? I can feel a real granddaddy of a headache coming on.'

Greg leaned forward and brushed her temple with his lips. 'Poor darling! You need a good man to take care of you.' His eyes teased mockingly, and she gave him a wry grimace.

'I *have*. Or have you forgotten?'

His teeth flashed as he smiled. 'Tony?'

'Yes—*Tony*.'

'Too tame for you, sweetie. You can't possibly be serious about him.'

'He's kind and considerate,' she defended slowly.

'So very logical,' he accorded without rancour. 'And such a solid basis for permanence.'

'Wretch!' she sighed ruefully.

Happily married with two children, Greg was serious about his work, but took delight in projecting an expected image. Over the years he had become a household name through lucrative television commercials, and he was one of a few whose exposure to the limelight hadn't affected him in any way.

'What are you two chatting about?' Leanne intervened, casting them both a suspicious frown. 'Shouldn't you be changed?' This to Lisa. 'We've been invited to join the sponsors for a drink. Roberto has accepted on our behalf.'

'Oh, *damn*,' Lisa muttered softly. 'I wanted to go home and soak in a hot bath for an hour.' She gave an audible groan. 'I'm supposed to be going out for dinner tonight.'

'Roberto—'

'I know,' she acknowledged with a rueful sigh. 'The royal command, no less. Five minutes,' she promised, moving towards the dressing-room, and on reaching it, she cast a glance over her shoulder. 'Two aspirin, Greg—I need them. Be a darling and find some.'

'Good as done.'

There was a single-bar electric heater which struggled to warm the chill winter air, but any good it achieved was mostly lost by virtue of a broken vent high on the wall. Lisa discarded her wrap and changed with skilled rapidity. It was one of Roberto's stipulations that each of his models wear up-to-the-minute clothes to any assignment, thus upholding the strict code of professionalism that had become his trademark. Consequently, when she emerged from the dressing-room she looked as if she was about to take the catwalk again.

'So at last you are ready.' The reproof was there, and she gave Roberto a singularly sweet smile.

'You want me to look my best, so don't be a bear.'

His thick eyebrows rose and almost disappeared into his brow. 'You're very beautiful, my darling,' he declared with heavy patience. 'But you will have to try harder. This afternoon your smile wasn't mirrored in the eyes.'

'A headache,' she explained, wrinkling her nose at him. He was a dear man, if a hard taskmaster. 'Greg is finding me some aspirin. I promise I shall shine brilliantly in a few minutes. Meanwhile, Susie and Leanne can cover for me.'

'Tomorrow—you will report to Sacha at ten.'

At once her eyes were alert, and she accepted the tumbler of water and two tablets Greg handed her, swallowing them before answering. 'Something unexpected? I thought I wouldn't be needed again until Friday.'

Roberto gave a satisfied smile. 'The price of popularity. Ten,' he reminded her. 'Don't be late.'

'Am I ever?'

'Ah, the young!' he derided musingly, shaking his head in weary rejection. 'Why is something so precious as youth wasted on them?'

Lisa slipped an arm through his and began leading the way towards the small flight of steps. 'Come, Papa bear,' she teased. 'A bright smile, any minute now—*voilà!*' She emerged into the main hall with a cheeky grin, and his husky laugh was lost in the rumbling chatter of the assembled crowd.

Within minutes she lifted a glass from a passing tray of drinks and raised it to her lips with dubious caution, then stifled a faint grimace. Under the guise of champagne it was little more than aerated cider.

'How long before we can decently make an exit, do you think?' she enquired of Greg.

'Fifteen minutes, if we're lucky,' he declared, then murmured beneath his breath, 'Oh-oh, we're about to be invaded!'

'Greg—darling! You were superb, as always.'

The owner of that husky voice was definitely a predatory female, from the shiny gloss covering her full petulant lips to the tips of her elegant Magli-shod feet. Lisa stayed where she was, a polite smile in place, despite the barbed glance she received in return.

With practised ease Greg dealt with his admirer—a blatant one at that, Lisa surmised, watching the avid expression evident in the woman's eyes. Pleasantly he refused her invitation, with just the right hint of regret tinging his voice, so that she was permitted to make a graceful exit without being a mark for her friends' spite.

'Very well done,' Lisa accorded softly, and caught his faint grimace.

'It's an occupational hazard.'

'She covets your body,' she teased wickedly, and incurred his wolfish grin.

'Unless I'm mistaken, here comes someone who covets *yours*.'

Now it was her turn to grimace. 'Don't you dare leave me!'

'Miss Gray.'

She turned at the sound of that faintly accented, deep drawl, and her eyes travelled up to meet Rick Andreas' enigmatic gaze. For an infinitesimal instant recognition flared, and with it a measure of hatred before she schooled her expression into a polite mask.

'Mr Andreas.' The acknowledgment bore little

accordance to civility, and a flicker of amused cynicism
pulled the edges of his sensuously-moulded mouth into a
mocking smile. For some inexplicable reason Lisa felt
suddenly breathless, and she found the fact annoying.
'What are you doing here?'

'I wasn't aware it was a private showing,' he countered
smoothly, and she seethed inwardly, barely aware of
Greg's interested gaze.

'Somehow I don't see a fashion show being something
commanding your—er—exalted presence,' she ventured sweetly, and sensed Greg's suppressed laughter.

One eyebrow rose in sardonic query. 'No? Is it unknown for one of the patrons of a particular charity to
view its fund-raising event?'

'Not at all,' she responded evenly, sparing him a
speaking glance. 'If that's the reason you're here.'

'Why else?'

Why else, *indeed*—if not to provide a palpable re-
minder of her diabolical position regarding James' predicament, and her own! 'In that case, if you'll excuse
me?' Her eyes dared him to detain her, and she could
have physically hit him when he reached out and caught
hold of her arm.

'It's time we left.' His glance skimmed towards Greg,
his smile a mere facsimile. 'If you will excuse us?'

His grip was merciless, and short of an unbecoming
display, there was little she could do that wouldn't
attract attention. 'I'm not going anywhere with you,' she
hissed vengefully, struggling to pull her arm free. 'Will
you let me go!'

'A tiff, you understand?'

Lisa heard the words, and didn't believe her ears.
How *dared* he? And Greg was smiling, his eyes openly

teasing as he cast her an amused glance before swinging towards the man at her side.

'The only way to effectively shut a woman's mouth is to cover it—with your own,' he murmured.

'That's an interesting thought,' Rick Andreas drawled.

'The *hell* it is,' she spluttered indignantly. It was bad enough having him as her aggressor, without Greg taking his side! 'I have a date this evening.'

'So you have,' Rick Andreas concurred smoothly. 'With me.'

'Never!'

His look quelled her at a glance, and Lisa thought she might well explode. 'If you don't let go of me this—*instant*, I swear I'll scream!'

'Try it.'

The atmosphere between them was electric. She opened her mouth to speak, then gave a silent gasp as his head lowered down to hers, and there was little she could do to escape his mouth's descent. Shocked disbelief kept her lips parted, and nothing prepared her for his ravaging possession. The kiss seared as it plundered to her very soul, tripping the rate of her pulse so that it accelerated to a hitherto unknown beat. It was a total annihilation, as he meant it to be, and she almost swayed when he released her.

'You—bastard!' Lisa whispered, her face pale, and the corners of his mouth took on a mocking slant.

'Such a harsh insult from such beautiful lips.' His eyes were dark and menacing, silently daring her to emit further vilification.

'Greg?' It was a last-ditch appeal, and she knew it.

'Much as I want to jump to your rescue, sweetie, the

man does appear to have some prior claim,' he said regretfully. 'How can I argue with that?'

'That's just the point,' she disclaimed vehemently. 'He *doesn't*!'

A slight frown furrowed Greg's brow. 'Do you deny you know the guy?'

'We shared dinner last evening,' Rick Andreas informed him, and Greg cast her a doubtful glance.

'Is that true?'

'Yes. *Yes!* But it's not what you think,' she wailed.

'Darling, what do you want me to do?' Greg arched with droll humour, and she endeavoured not to explode.

'Tell him to leave me alone!'

Greg gave the man before him a long considering look, then slowly shook his head. 'He's bigger than I am.' A slow grin broke from his lips. 'Besides, you look good together.'

'My God,' Lisa whispered in subdued fury, 'I asked you to beat him, not join him!'

Rick Andreas' teeth gleamed white as he taunted softly, 'Is there anyone else you want to call to your rescue?'

She surveyed him with stark animosity. 'You surely can't expect me to simply leave here with you?'

'Why ever not?' he parried in a low drawl, and she retaliated without thought,

'Give me one reason why I should?'

He regarded her thoughtfully, and she could have screamed at the time it took him to speak. 'I think you already know the answer to that.'

Her eyes met his unwaveringly for what seemed an age, then she slowly dropped her gaze. Turning slightly towards Greg, she murmured, 'Convey my farewells to

Roberto, will you?' Without a further word she turned and moved down the hall, oblivious to the sea of faces either side as she made her way to the exit.

In the adjoining parking area she crossed to where her car stood and delved into her bag for the key. A lean muscular hand closed over hers, and she looked up angrily. 'What now?'

'You're coming with me,' Rick Andreas instructed quietly.

'The hell I am!'

'Obviously an essential spanking was omitted from your upbringing,' he drawled.

She glared at him. 'Next, you'll tell me you intend remedying that!'

'Now there's an evocative thought.'

Her chin lifted fractionally, and her brown eyes darkened with renewed anger. 'I presume your sudden interest in fashion modelling is merely an excuse to inspect the merchandise,' she declared, allowing her gaze to sweep him from head to foot with hateful enmity. 'Well, I've just completed *mine*, and I don't like what I see,' she concluded, becoming incensed by his sardonic mockery. 'Oh, go take a running *jump*!'

She wrenched free of his grasp—all too easily, she was to reflect later. Shaky fingers unlocked the door, then she slid in behind the wheel. A deft twist of her wrist fired the engine, then she shifted the gear stick and drove off without so much as a backward glance.

CHAPTER THREE

LISA hadn't been inside her apartment an hour when the phone rang, and she looked at it in silent antipathy, hardly wanting to answer it. After the twelfth peal she slowly lifted the receiver.

'Lisa? Thank God! I've been trying to locate you.'

James. Who else? she grimaced ruefully, with no need to guess the reason for his call.

'Where have you been?'

Her fingers tightened their hold on the receiver until the knuckles turned white. 'Participating in a fashion show, remember?' she attempted lightly, and heard his indrawn breath.

'Has Andreas contacted you?'

She hesitated, feeling loath to reveal more than was necessary about what had transpired with the hateful Greek. 'I saw him this afternoon,' she informed him noncommittally.

'Oh?' James appeared genuinely surprised, and she wondered if Rick Andreas' appearance at the fashion show had been coincidental, after all. 'Have you reached a decision?'

The conversation was rapidly assuming nightmarish proportion, and Lisa took a deep steadying breath. 'How would you react if I were to refuse his proposition?'

A cataclysmic silence reverberated down the line. 'I

can appreciate your reluctance,' he managed at last, and she could almost sense him slump back in his chair.

Damn—*damn* her stupid temper! The consequences of her outburst had done little else but haunt her ever since she'd driven off from the car park in a rage. There was only one solution, and she spoke aloud before she had time to change her mind. 'Do you have—' she forced herself to use his name—'Rick's phone number? He neglected to give it to me, and it's imperative I speak with him tonight.'

'Can't it wait until tomorrow? I only have a number where he can be reached during the day.'

'No, I'm afraid not.' She daren't give Rick Andreas time to put the wheels in motion, for there was little doubt that he would. It had to be *now*.

'He may have a private listing,' James pondered slowly, and she could almost sense his frown. 'In which case it will be impossible to get the number from the exchange.'

'Surely you must know someone who has his address, at least,' she insisted, praying that he did. If not, there was little hope she could prevent the inevitable.

'He lives in Vaucluse, that much I know. I'll make a few calls, and get back to you as soon as I can.'

It was more than an hour before the phone rang, and by then Lisa was a mess of nerves.

'His phone number is a closely guarded secret, but I have an address,' James revealed abruptly. 'I don't suppose you'll tell me what all this is about?'

She drew a shaky breath. 'Trust me.' His irritation was conveyed by a long-drawn-out sigh, and she hurriedly wrote down the address he gave. 'Thanks, James.' With scant regard for his curiosity she replaced the receiver, then quickly crossed to her bedroom and caught up a coat from the wardrobe.

Extracting keys from her bag, she moved to the front door, locked it behind her, then crossed the corridor to summon the elevator.

Her movements were jerky and hurried, accentuated by her inner tension. Having to eat humble pie would be no mean feat, and every nerve-end screamed in angry rejection.

In the car she turned on the heater, and it wasn't until she was on the road that she began to feel its effect. Traffic travelling towards the city was fairly dense, and she drove automatically, utilising all her concentration as she negotiated the route to the prestigous hillside suburb that afforded a fairytale view of the inner harbour and city. Lights in the distance provided a delicate tracery against the inky backdrop of a night-time sky, and kaleidoscopic flashing neon atop towering office buildings added movement and colour to a teeming metropolis.

The street's location wasn't difficult to find, and Lisa eased the car to a halt adjacent an imposing set of gates. Minutes later a single oath slipped from her lips as she discovered they were locked.

A closer inspection revealed an intercom system set into one of the concrete pillars, and she depressed the button, stating her name and a desire to see the head of the house.

There was the click of a switch, then a deep slightly accented voice declared with the utmost civility, 'Mr Andreas is out for the evening.'

It was an unforeseen complication that Lisa inwardly cursed. If he was out wining and dining, she could have a lengthy wait ahead of her. 'May I come in and wait?'

There was a slight pause. 'I have instructions not to release the gates until Mr Andreas' return.'

'I don't suppose you have any idea when he's expected?'

'I am unable to say.'

A long sigh escaped her lips. 'Thank you.'

She turned and walked back to the Mazda, slipping in behind the wheel to sit in solitary silence as she contemplated just how long her lonely vigil might be. A glance at her watch showed it was almost nine. With luck she'd have no more than an hour or two to fill.

The car radio provided some light relief, but as time dragged on she began to get restless, wanting the evening over and done with so that whatever the outcome, she could at least go home to bed. Rick Andreas' reaction to her presence here at this hour of the night didn't bear thinking about, and she wondered at her own temerity.

At some stage she must have dozed off to sleep, for she woke with a start, suddenly alert to the slight sound that had disturbed her lapse into somnolence.

A car had pulled up in front of the gates, its powerful headlights providing a broad illumination, and even as she watched the gates swung open by remote control and the car moved forward.

Scarcely pausing to think, Lisa slid from her car and ran to the gates, managing to slip through an instant before they closed.

Well, at least she was in the grounds, and with a deep sigh she braced herself for the unenviable confrontation, setting out with brisk determined steps along the gently curving driveway.

Seconds later she froze as a deep menacing growl up ahead rapidly transcended into a threatening spine-chilling bark that was joined by another, and she stood electrified as two Dobermann Pinschers bounded towards her.

She must have screamed. Her mouth parted, but she had no recollection of emitting a sound, and for a heart-stopping second she closed her eyes against what seemed an inevitable attack.

Dimly she heard a sharp command, followed by the whining protest of the dogs as they stood guard until their master identified the intruder and dismissed them with a harsh oath.

'You little *fool*!' Rick Andreas snapped savagely. 'They're trained to attack and maim!'

'If I'd known in advance the welcome I would receive, believe me, I'd never have come,' Lisa told him shakily. In the shadowed half-light he looked angry—furiously so, she amended as a frisson of fear slithered icily down her spine.

'What the hell are you doing here at this hour of the night?'

'I have to talk to you,' she began half-heartedly, and glimpsed the glitter of pitiless disregard in those ebony depths.

'I was unaware that we have anything to discuss.'

'Couldn't we go inside?' She cast him a desperate glance as the night's shadows appeared to loom even closer. The chill wintry air seeped through her clothes and she shivered.

'Beard the lion's den, so to speak?' he drawled cynically, thrusting his hands into the pockets of his sheepskin-lined car coat. 'Are you sure that's wise?'

It mightn't be wise, but she had no other choice. 'I'd feel happier out of reach of your guard dogs.'

'Properly introduced, they become docile and friendly.'

She cast him a look of disbelief. 'You're joking.' She was still inwardly shaking from the encounter, and was loath to put his statement to the test.

With a mocking gesture he swept his arm towards the front door, and it was with some trepidation that she preceded him past its carved panels into an impressive foyer.

The warmth of central heating reached out and enveloped her, and she felt extremely vulnerable as he closed the door. Turning towards her he bade brusquely,

'Come into the lounge. I'll get you a drink.'

Lisa felt in need of something to calm her frazzled nerves, and she followed him into a large spacious room that was elegantly furnished and tastefully decorated.

'Sit down.' He crossed to a well-stocked bar and extracted two glasses. 'Brandy?' At her silent acquiescing nod he placed ice into each glass and followed it with a generous measure of spirit before moving back to her side. 'Drink it down. You look as if you're still suffering from shock.'

It was a command she thought it best to heed, and she sipped the contents slowly, feeling it run like liquid fire through her veins.

Rick Andreas remained standing, and she watched as he swirled the liquid in his glass with seeming deliberation before fixing her with a raking stare.

'So,' he began in a voice that was dangerously soft, 'what is the reason for this visit?'

She closed her eyes momentarily in an attempt at

composure. 'I lost my temper this afternoon,' she offered slowly, and he hazarded dryly,

'An apology or an explanation?'

Lisa met his gaze unflinchingly. 'I've had the opportunity to reconsider your proposition.'

'Indeed?' he arched sardonically.

The cynical gleam apparent in his dark eyes was too much for her, and she glanced at a point to the right of his shoulder. 'I've decided to accept.'

He was silent for so long her nerves almost reached screaming point.

'You are aware that the deadline for your decision was more than seven hours ago?'

She swallowed the lump that had suddenly risen in her throat. 'Are you telling me your offer is no longer applicable?'

'As I remember, you refused it in no uncertain terms.'

'Oh, for heaven's sake!' she exclaimed emotively. 'James informed me of your ultimatum over lunch to-day—*yesterday*,' she corrected. 'Within a matter of hours you appeared on the scene and began dictating to me like some—feudal *tyrant!* How did you expect me to react?'

He regarded her silently for what seemed an age, and it took considerable courage to hold his gaze.

'I'm prepared to "cement the linking chain"—your words, I believe,' she declared evenly, 'by entering into a marriage of convenience.'

'Convenience?' One eyebrow slanted sardonically. 'Make no mistake, Lisa. Not only do I want a wife by my side—I need a woman in my bed.' His lips twisted with wry cynicism. 'Impossible to believe you could be so naïve as to think otherwise.'

Her eyes flared with helpless anger. 'You're totally despicable!' she choked.

'I've been called worse,' he declared imperturbably, and without thought Lisa drained her glass and stood to her feet.

'I don't think I can bear to stay in this room—this house, a moment longer!'

'Oh, come now,' Rick drawled. 'Have another drink. We should toast our—alliance.'

'One was quite enough,' she answered stoically. 'I have to drive home.'

'I'll see you reach your apartment safely.'

'No—thank you.'

'Such independence!' he mocked cynically. 'Do you intend displaying such a wealth of it after our marriage?'

'Will you let me?' Lisa parried, and incurred a dark probing look.

'I won't tolerate disobedience.'

'My God!' she burst out incautiously, her fine brown eyes flashing with anger. 'What do you intend? This—mansion is like a fortress!' She swept him from head to toe with a wrathful glare. 'Am I to be confined within its gates like some sort of slave in a harem?'

His lips twisted into a cynical smile that held a hint of cruelty, and his eyes held no humour at all. 'You possess a vivid imagination.'

'I won't become subjugated to you in any way,' she insisted vengefully.

'Don't begin adding qualifications,' Rick declared dangerously, and she erupted into angry speech.

'Accept me as I am, or not at all!'

His eyes glittered with ruthless disregard. 'You're hardly in a position to bargain.'

Her head tilted of its own volition, and there was the light of battle in her gaze. 'I won't bow down to the dictates of an egotistical, chauvinistic male!' The brandy was putting words in her mouth that she normally would think twice about uttering. 'I'll fight you, Rick Andreas—every inch of the way!'

'I don't relish comparing our marriage to a battle-field,' he told her inexorably. 'Take heed, my foolish child. When it comes to an arsenal, my weapons are far superior to any you can summon.'

'I'm neither foolish, nor a child,' Lisa flared, fixing him with a chilling glare.

'Very much both,' Rick accorded grimly, and she moved in an attempt to brush past him.

'I'm going home.'

'I'll drive you.'

'The hell you will!' she expostulated, hating his implacability, and she struggled impotently as he reached out and caught her arms, holding her still with an ease that was galling. 'Get your hands off me,' she snapped furiously. 'You don't own me yet!'

'But I have more than an option on the merchandise,' he declared mercilessly, and reaching out he curved hard hands over her shoulders, pulling her close.

She wanted to rage and scream against fate for putting her in such an invidious position, but resorted instead to overt flippancy. 'What is this—*rape*?'

For a moment she thought she had goaded him too far, and she felt inexplicably frightened of the consequences. His face was set, carved into an angry mask, and she shuddered as his head lowered down to hers.

The mouth that covered her own effected a bruising punishment, and a despairing moan burned her throat as he forced her lips apart, violating the soft inner tissue as he initiated a brutal assault on her senses.

She tried to escape, but each and every attempt proved fruitless as she beat her fists against his back, his ribs—anywhere she could reach. Even a few tricks she had learnt as a means of self-defence failed miserably, and she became locked into a timeless void, lapsing into reluctant passivity as he wreaked havoc with her tortured emotions.

After what seemed an eternity the pressure eased, and she almost swayed as he lifted his head. Strangely, she wanted to cry. To have this final humiliation was almost more than she could endure, and stupid tears welled, making her eyes look like huge drowning pools.

Through a watery mist she glimpsed the grim implacability reflected in his harsh features and suppressed a shiver. 'I'd like to go home,' she declared emotionlessly. Her lips felt swollen, and she could taste her own blood.

Without a word he took her elbow and led her towards the front door, ascending the steps to where his car stood parked on the driveway. Opening the door, he said curtly, 'Get in.'

Lisa felt too enervated to defy him. All her former fire had deserted her, and with a gesture of defeat she slipped into the passenger seat.

During the thirty minutes it took to reach her apartment neither spoke a word, and the instant the car drew to a halt in the courtyard she reached for the doorclasp.

'Just a moment.'

Lisa turned wearily to face him. 'I must get some sleep. I have an early photographic session.'

'What time will you finish?'

'Why?'

'We'll have lunch together,' Rick declared, and she returned waspishly,

'I don't particularly want to meet you for lunch.'

'Doubtless if you had your way, the next time we meet would be at the register office,' he drawled, and she gave a long-drawn-out sight.

'Which will be *when*?'

The lighted courtyard threw strange shadows over the planes of his face, making them appear vaguely satanical. 'As soon as it can be arranged. Within a few days, at most.'

'Heaven help me!' Lisa sighed piously.

'Doubtful.'

'Of course,' she concurred with seeming sweetness, '*Hell* is far more appropriate.'

'It is to your advantage to be realistic,' he slanted with wry cynicism, and she muttered,

'Nothing in this damnable scheme is to my advantage!'

'Oh, come—it can't be all bad.'

Her eyes sparked with ill-concealed anger. 'What irks me unbearably is the fact that you've stipulated I must be part of your diabolical deal. Surely there must be some law that forbids coercion of one human being by another!'

'You want to change your mind?'

The query was dangerously soft, and she shivered at its implication. 'I can't,' she declared hollowly.

'Then I suggest you refrain from behaving like a recalcitrant child and face the inevitable,' Rick determined hardily.

Perhaps she was, she reflected tiredly. Maybe tomorrow she'd view the entire thing in a different light. 'I'm going inside,' she informed him stoically, and reaching for the doorclasp she slid out and made her way unhurriedly towards the main entrance. She slipped her key into the lock, then secured the door behind her without giving the waiting car or the man at its wheel another glance.

Sleep didn't come easily, and when the alarm pealed a few hours later she switched it off with a despairing groan, then slumped back against her pillow and put a hand to her throbbing head.

Never in the past few years had she felt less inclined to face the photographic camera, or its demanding operator. For five blissful minutes she contemplated calling Roberto and telling him she couldn't make it, then loyalty surfaced, and she swept the bedcovers aside and made for the shower.

After breakfasting on toast and black coffee she rang for a taxi, then added the finishing touches to her make-up. She was about to leave the apartment when the phone pealed and she crossed quickly to pick up the receiver.

'Lisa? I've been trying to get hold of you—last night, and this morning. Why didn't you answer?'

Damn, damn, *damn*! She took a deep calming breath and responded evenly, 'I can't talk now, James. I'm just on my way out. I'll ring you this evening.' She replaced the receiver before he had the opportunity to squeeze in a further word.

No sooner had she moved three steps than the phone rang again. The temptation to ignore it was strong, but common sense prevailed, and she snatched up the receiver and all but snarled into it.

'Good grief, what side of the bed did you get out of this morning?'

Tony! This was rapidly digressing into a comedic farce! 'The wrong side, obviously,' she declared with unaccustomed irritability. 'What do you want?'

'What have I done?' he demanded. 'First, I get a call from James cancelling our dinner date on your behalf, then this morning you snap like a fretful lioness when I merely wanted to enquire about your health, and invite you to lunch.'

'I can't meet you for lunch.' Having to explain why seemed beyond her at that precise moment. A quick glance at her watch determined that her taxi would have had ample time to arrive. 'Look, I have to dash. I'll catch up with you later.'

Rick Andreas had a hell of a lot to answer for, she muttered furiously as she closed the door of her apartment. Without waiting for the elevator, she made for the stairs and flew down them with graceful agility, reaching the entrance foyer within minutes to glimpse her taxi parked in the courtyard.

Sacha was even more demanding than usual, his comments and directions caustic to a degree where Lisa was tempted to respond in kind.

'Darling, you are *limp*, for God's sake! *Smile*—imagine you're lying supine on the golden sands of the French Riviera, or the Costa del Sol.'

Her expression became slightly sceptical. 'In the middle of a southern hemispheric winter? Somehow my mind refuses to comply.'

'*Pretend*, why don't you? The sun is warm, the sea is blue, and your lover is anointing your body with oil. Close your eyes, think about it—then open them slowly and look at me,' Sacha commanded. 'Ah, that's better. And again. Good girl! Now sit up, knees raised, ankles together. That's it. Roberto—the hat. Yes, that's it. More of an angle. Pick up the glass and sip from the straw. Okay. Change position. Lean back, head towards the camera—sultry, darling, is the look I want.'

How much longer before Sacha would call a halt? Another hour? Wearily she complied with his direction, endeavouring to achieve the desired effect.

'Go and change, darling.' Sensing her fatigue, he gave a faint smile. 'Half an hour should wrap it up.'

Lisa rose to her feet and made for the dressing-room, slipping out of the one-piece suit with the ease of long practice, then she collected the two silky scraps of material from Millie's outstretched hands, and cast the older woman a wry grimace. 'This is a bikini?' she queried sceptically as she tied the shoestring straps in place. 'It's more like an apology for one!'

'You can wear it. Few could,' Millie assured her with a comforting smile, and Lisa raised her eyes heavenward, then wrinkled her nose in an attempt at humour.

'At least I'm only facing the camera. If I was supposed to take the catwalk attired like this, I think I'd opt out! Surely the designer can't expect to actually sell something as brief as this?'

'Thousands of girls would give their eye-teeth to possess a figure such as yours,' Millie assured. 'They see you splashed in fashion magazines and attempt to copy by buying whatever you model.' She gave a philosophical shrug. 'It's the name of the game.'

'My, my,' Lisa drawled, 'you are in a cynical mood!'

'No, just honest.' Millie gestured towards the door. 'Now, get out there before Sacha starts bellowing. He's like a bear with a sore head this morning.'

Some time later, her temper almost frayed, Lisa

attempted yet again one of Sacha's barked commands, and when she turned towards him she saw Rick Andreas' lengthy frame leaning with indolent ease against the door jamb.

Her eyes widened in startled surprise, then narrowed as she darted a quick glance towards the photographer. An audience at any time was strictly forbidden, and she waited for his reaction.

'That will do,' Sacha dismissed with a curt nod, and Lisa cast Roberto an enquiring look, then swung her attention to the man who was an interloper amongst professionals.

Rick Andreas didn't move, and it took considerable aplomb to remain unruffled as his eyes made a slow deliberate appraisal over her scantily-clad figure.

'What are you doing here?' she demanded ungraciously, feeling positively *naked* beneath his assessing gaze. Her wrap was within reach, and she caught it up and slipped her arms into it, belting the ties about her waist with hands that shook.

'We have a luncheon date, remember?' he drawled, and she cast him a hateful glance.

'Couldn't you have waited outside?' Unconsciously her eyes slid towards the photographer.

'Sacha and I go back a long way,' Rick intimated ambiguously. 'I have permission to invade his sanctum.'

He was amused, darn him! Well, two could play at that game. Effecting a mock curtsy, Lisa moved towards the dressing-room. 'You must be privileged,' she murmured with scant politeness. 'Now, if you'll kindly step aside, I'll change into something more suitable.'

He reached out and trailed his fingers along the edge of her collarbone towards the hollow at the base of her throat, allowing them to rest there for a mere second before following a downward path to where the silken vee of her wrap crossed the gentle swell of her breasts. 'I much prefer the way you are,' he murmured, a teasing smile slanting his sensuous mouth. 'But in public, you'd create a riot.'

Oh, he was *impossible*! Her eyes sparked with silent fury, then mindful of two pairs of interested eyes, she stepped round him and moved into the relative privacy of the dressing-room.

'We've finished for the morning,' Lisa informed him, and on meeting Millie's startled eyes she gave a disparaging grimace. 'Thank God! Sacha has been almost impossible to please.' She slipped off the wrap and slid her fingers up to untie the thin straps behind her neck.

Ten minutes later she was dressed, the fine wool skirt with its matching jacket over a tailored silk blouse the epitome of elegance. High-heeled shoes in finest kid graced her slim feet, and she smoothed a hand over her hair to ensure there were no untidy wisps escaping from the graceful chignon. Make-up was kept to a minimum with a light dusting of powder, the application of eye-shadow and mascara, with lipgloss covering her natural shade of lipstick.

Lisa moved out into the studio to see the three men together in conversation, and as she neared them Roberto beckoned her to his side.

'We were just discussing you.'

'Oh?' Her surprise was genuine. 'Am I permitted to ask why?'

'The fact that you've just completed your final assignment,' Rick informed her irrefutably, adding with deceptive calm, 'photographically, as well as fashion-wise.'

Indignation spiralled to assume barely concealed anger. 'I refuse to believe you're serious!'

His eyes took on a dangerous gleam. 'Believe it, Lisa,' he declared hardily, and she retaliated without thought.

'I'm not giving up my career!'

His expression hardened, becoming frighteningly implacable, and an icy frisson feathered its way down her spine. 'You just have.'

'Oh, I see.' The words poured from her in an angry flood. 'All previous associations must be severed.'

A muscle tautened along his jaw, and she wondered at her own sanity in attempting to cross him. He had already proved he was indomitable in every way, and her actions could only bring retribution on her hapless head.

'Not at all,' Rick drawled. 'Merely that your working career is at an end.'

Lisa glanced towards Roberto, then skimmed to Sacha. 'There are assignments, at least two fashion shows that have been extensively advertised—with me taking part,' she breathed shakily. 'How will you manage?'

Sacha gave an expressive shrug. 'There are others who can take your place. Perhaps not as well. But the show will go on.'

It wasn't what she'd expected to hear, and she sought reassurance. 'Roberto?'

'You're the tops, sweetheart,' he said gently, spreading his hands in an expressive gesture. 'Sacha is right— everyone in this particular field is expendable.' He gave her a wolfish grin. 'If you were my personal property, I wouldn't want you on display for every male to feast his avid gaze upon, either.'

It was contrived sabotage at best, and the look she cast Rick held bitter animosity. 'I don't suppose it will do any good if I ask you to relent?'

'No.' The monosyllable held grim inflexibility, and with an impotent shrug she turned towards Roberto.

'What now? A farewell drink?' She laughed hollowly. 'Or do I receive the golden handshake?'

'Champagne,' Sacha told her with droll humour. 'I have some on ice.'

'Very convenient!' There was nothing she could do to mask the faint bitterness in her voice, and the photographer gave a lopsided smile as he retrieved a bottle and five glasses from the small refrigerator.

Millie joined them, and Lisa sipped the sparkling ambrosia rather more quickly than perhaps she should in an attempt to dull the edges. The Lord knew she needed something to bolster her sadly deflated morale! With idle satisfaction she felt the warm tingle in her veins as the alcohol began to take rapid effect.

Without her being aware of it, the small group had somehow reassembled themselves, for Rick stood by her side, far too close for comfort. She was suddenly shockingly aware of his presence, the faint musky aroma of his aftershave and the sheer animal magnetism he projected. Her eyes seemed drawn to his rough-hewn features, and her heart began an erratic beat as she let her gaze rest on his wide sensuous mouth. Remembering its touch made her shiver, and with a sense of desperation she allowed Roberto to replenish her glass.

'I suppose you've arranged all the details?' she remarked with a seeming smile the instant Roberto was out of earshot. 'You appear to have taken care of everything else.'

'Did you doubt that I would?' Rick drawled enigmatically, and her smile widened.

'Of course not, darling. You're the quintessence of efficiency.'

His eyes narrowed fractionally, taking in the twin peaks of colour high on her cheekbones. 'Tell me, did you eat breakfast?'

'I really can't remember,' she declared, a slight frown of concentration creasing her brow. 'No, now that I come to think of it.'

'In that case, you'd better let me finish the contents of that glass.' He reached out and took it from her fingers, and her lips parted in silent rebuke. 'Don't defy me,' he warned. 'You wouldn't like the consequences.'

'My goodness!' she exclaimed with simulated horror. 'If you attempt to threaten me before we're married, whatever will you do afterwards?'

Without a word Rick downed the remaining liquid in her glass, then finished his own. 'If you'll excuse us?' His glance encompassed the three people in the room. 'We have a reservation for lunch.' He caught hold of her arm and propelled her towards the door.

'I'll ring you,' Lisa called from the aperture, then they were in the corridor and heading for the elevator.

'You arrogant *bastard*!' she snapped furiously. 'Did you have to haul me away like that?'

'Watch your foolhardy tongue,' Rick cautioned silkily.

'Why?' she demanded with a trace of belligerence. 'What will you do?'

The look he gave her was ruthlessly intense. 'Silence it.'

'I don't appreciate caveman tactics,' she flung, hating

him at that moment as she'd never hated anyone before.

'Then don't tempt me to use them.'

The elevator arrived, the doors sliding open with smooth electronic precision, and she stepped inside, feeling stifled in the enclosed space, intensely aware of the man at her side.

'Where are we eating?'

He slanted her a wry glance. 'I don't imagine it matters much. The important thing is to provide you with food.'

'I'm not a toddler in need of a restraining hand,' Lisa declared as he caught hold of her elbow. A humourless laugh escaped her lips. 'Or perhaps you consider me inebriated?'

His faint smile was wholly cynical as they reached the pavement and vied with fellow pedestrians. 'Just the slightest—yes.'

'Are you usually so flagrantly blunt?'

His eyes took on a dangerous gleam. 'Be a good girl, hmn? We're nearly there.'

'What will you do if I'm not?' Some devilish imp appeared to have hold of her tongue, and she watched in idle fascination as he bit off an angry epithet.

'Take you back to your apartment, and give you the lesson you deserve.'

'Dear me—under threat of violence, what other course is left but to comply?'

The look he cast her almost withered her on the spot, and she didn't offer a further word as he led her into an exclusive eatery.

Small and intimate, the service appeared excellent from the speed with which the first course was put on the table. She had no recollection of ordering, and by the time the main course arrived, she was feeling considerably less lightheaded.

'When do we exchange our vows?'

'You are anxious to become Lisa *Andreas*?' Rick mocked, and she glanced down at her plate at the implication those words evoked.

'You know the answer to that,' she managed quietly. 'But I'd like to be informed as to the where and when of it.'

His gaze was startlingly direct. 'Four o'clock, Friday afternoon.'

Disbelief widened her eyes into large dark pools of incredulity. 'Not this—'

'The day after tomorrow,' Rick concurred levelly, and she broke into incoherent speech.

'You can't possibly have arranged everything so quickly—it takes three days at least, doesn't it? I can't marry you so soon.' An audible groan left her lips. 'I haven't even told Tony I can't marry *him*!'

'Then I suggest you do so at the earliest opportunity.'

'You don't give a damn, do you?' she lashed out angrily.

'How you discard this—*friend*, is entirely your affair,' he projected with icy fatalism.

'What if he's my lover?' The words slipped out without thought, and she saw his eyes harden momentarily, then assume sardonic mockery.

'I don't imagine you'll remember him for long.'

'You—you barbaric—*savage*!' Lisa stumbled in utter loathing.

'Because I dare to suggest I can dispense with his image?' he queried cynically.

'Compared to your considerable experience, Tony is just a callow youth, I suppose?'

'Do you doubt it?'

How could she? There was a whole lifetime of living reflected in the depths of those dark eyes. The knowledge made her feel strangely vulnerable, and she let her gaze fall.

'I can't eat any more.' It was true, her appetite had vanished.

His eyes gave her a raking scrutiny, then he offered silkily, 'Have some coffee, while I finish.' He signalled a waiter and placed an order, then resumed eating.

Lisa sat in silence, sipping the hot aromatic brew when it arrived with scarce enjoyment. Her headache had returned with a vengeance, rapidly transcending from a niggling throb to a giant-size ache. Automatically she reached into her bag for some painkillers, extracted two from a vial, and reached for a glass of water.

'It might help if you finished your meal,' Rick remarked dryly, and she glanced across the table to find his eyes regarding her with compelling scrutiny.

'It would choke in my throat!'

'You don't eat sufficient food to satisfy a sparrow.'

'On the basis of having shared two meals with me, you dare judge?' Her brown eyes deepened with anger. 'I watch my weight. In my profession I have to, but I do it sensibly, and supplement each meal with prescribed vitamins.'

'You no longer have a profession, remember?'

'Thanks to you!'

'Drink your coffee,' he instructed brusquely, folding his napkin, and she shot him a venomous glare. 'There are a few formalities we have to attend to, then I'm taking you home.'

'Yours, or mine?' she quipped without thought, and incurred his deep slanting glance.

'Yours, eventually,' he declared imperturbably. 'We're dining out tonight.'

'Do you usually command?' Lisa queried indignantly. 'I prefer to be asked.'

'And give you the opportunity to refuse?'

'Oh, what does it matter,' she sighed. 'You'll win in the end.'

'Sensible of you to realise it.'

She cast him a look of utter loathing. 'Can we leave? If I stay here a moment longer, I'll probably say something totally regrettable!'

There were stupid angry tears clouding her vision as they reached the pavement, and she was too enervated to attempt wrenching her arm from his steel-like grasp as he led the way to a nearby underground car park.

CHAPTER FOUR

THE ensuing hour proved frenetic as Rick insisted she bear evidence of their intended liaison by forcing her to accept a row of diamonds set in platinum, despite angry protestation, and he slid the magnificent ring on to her finger.

Next came an appointment with the head of a legal firm.

'A legal technicality,' Rick explained brusquely as they entered a prestigious office block and crossed to the elevator.

Lisa felt her stomach lurch at the implication. 'You want me to sign some form of document?' she queried incredulously, and incurred his curt nod.

'Stating that you are entering into our proposed marriage willingly, and without duress.' His expression became ruthlessly inflexible. 'It will also preclude instigation of divorce proceedings for a minimum period.'

She looked at him in stunned disbelief. 'It would never stand up in a court of law,' she whispered shakily.

'It's a form of insurance,' he insisted pitilessly. 'At the end of five years, should a divorce be mutually desirable, I'll agree to a settlement—' he named a sum that made her gasp, and she swept her lashes wide to regard him with animosity.

'You believe in covering all the angles, don't you?'

His dark probing look was hard and merciless. 'I'm a

wealthy man, and I haven't attained success by being a fool.'

Lisa had difficulty controlling her temper. 'Nice to know you have such faith in human nature! By taking such blatant precautions, you obviously suspect I'll marry and run—to the nearest lawyer to fleece you for every cent I can get.'

'It has been done before,' Rick declared dryly, and she burst into angry speech.

'Aren't you forgetting something? It was *you* who insisted on marriage.' Her eyes sparked alive with barely contained fury. 'I'm merely the *pawn* in this diabolical scheme!'

'You'll be adequately compensated. A generous clothing allowance, travel—among other things,' he told her silkily. 'And at the end of it, a generous settlement.'

It was the 'other things' that bothered her! 'Five years of being your concubine. I doubt I'll last the distance,' she muttered darkly.

'Who knows?' he quirked indolently. 'You may decide to make it a lifetime commitment.'

'Impossible!'

'Here's the elevator,' Rick declared smoothly, and she preceded him into the enclosed space with the movements of an automaton.

'What if I refuse to sign?' Her expression was wholly serious, and his eyes narrowed imperceptibly.

'I've already made one allowance. I won't make another.'

Despite the warmth of artificial heating Lisa felt suddenly cold, and when they reached the designated floor she managed to project a semblance of civility as she gave her assurance she understood the ramifications of the document presented for signature.

It began to rain as Rick negotiated traffic on the Harbour Bridge, and the stormy skies seemed to magnify her precarious mercurial mood. By the time the Ferrari came to a halt outside her apartment block the heavens had emptied, providing a deluge.

Without thought, Lisa automatically undid her seatbelt and slid from her seat, breaking into a run as the rain began to soak through her clothes.

'Little fool!' Rick remarked bleakly as he came up behind her.

She effected an uncaring shrug as he jabbed the button to summon the elevator. 'I don't consider it's necessary for you to escort me direct to my door.' She turned and thrust him an icy glare. 'I think I've had about as much of you as I can stand. If you force me to spend this evening in your company, I'll probably throw up!'

'Behave,' he insisted hardily, grasping her arm in an ungentle grip as she turned towards the stairs.

Furiously she rounded on him, her expression incredibly angry. 'Let me go, damn you!'

'Try my patience much further, and I won't be answerable for the consequences,' he growled, and she shot him a quelling glare.

'You'd hit a woman?'

'There are more subtle forms of punishment.'

The warning was there, and she shivered at the open threat of it. What on earth was wrong with her, goading him to such an extent?

They reached her apartment, and she slid open her bag, delving for the slim holder containing a variety of keys. Extracting it, she selected the correct key and handed it to him without so much as a word.

Once inside, she slipped off her shoes, then her coat. 'I could do with a drink.' She needed something to quieten her inner rage. It consumed her, making her want to lash out at anything within reach.

'Do you think that's wise?'

Studiously ignoring him, she crossed to the kitchen and opened a cupboard. 'Whisky?'

'Ice, a splash of soda, if you have it—otherwise water,' Rick said dryly, watching as she opened the refrigerator.

Lisa felt his eyes on her, and shrugged her shoulders in an effort to dispel the hairs prickling the length of her spine. Turning, she solemnly handed him the glass, challenging with deliberate emphasis, 'Here's to our— er—future.' She took a generous swallow, then grimaced with distaste. 'This is almost as revolting as I expect our marriage to be!'

'Give it up, Lisa,' he warned dangerously, and she slanted him a look of mock incredulity.

'Surely the document I've just signed makes the actual ceremony a mere formality?'

The look he cast her was dark and analytical. 'Aren't you in the least afraid I may take advantage of that fact?'

She lifted her glass and gulped down half the contents. 'Today, tomorrow—*Friday*. What difference does it make?' For a mere second her eyes became hauntingly vulnerable, then assumed glittery bitterness. 'You won't observe *my* feelings.'

Without a word he placed his glass down on to a nearby table and followed it with her own. As his intention became clear she took a backwards step, then

looked wildly for a means of escape. Hard hands caught
hold of her arms, bruising, as he impelled her relentlessly forward, and she began to struggle, fighting to be
free of him.

His mouth captured hers with a brutal savagery that
locked the breath in her throat. It was as if he was
determined to invade her soul, stamping his possession
in a manner that could leave no doubt as to his undis-
puted right to do so. The inner tissue of her mouth still
bore the force of his previous onslaught, and she whim-
pered as he heedlessly took his fill.

With a sudden gesture of disgust he thrust her to arm's
length, and his hands moved to close painfully over her
shoulders.

'You goad a man to the very limit of his endurance,' he
bit hardily, his dark eyes devoid of pity as they raked her
whitened features and settled on her faintly swollen
mouth. 'Be thankful I control a rein on my temper,' he
concluded bleakly. 'Otherwise, believe me, you
wouldn't now be standing on your feet.'

Lisa swallowed with difficulty. 'If that's lesson number
one,' she husked through numbed lips, 'I'll forgo all the
rest.' The pressure over her shoulders increased, making
her wince with pain. 'You're hurting me!'

His eyes glittered dangerously, then with a muttered
oath he let his hands fall to his sides and she swayed,
clutching hold of the nearest support in an effort to
steady herself, unaware in that agonising moment of
instability that she had caught hold of his arm, and when
realisation dawned she withdrew as if burnt.

His expression hardened and she gasped out loud as
his hands grasped her waist.

'Don't,' she uttered in an unconscious plea, and her

eyes clouded, then became veiled. 'I don't think I could bear any more!'

'Look at me,' Rick commanded harshly, and when she didn't obey he lifted a hand to her chin and tilted it. 'Lisa?'

At the deep threat in his voice she slowly lifted her lashes, sweeping them wide to meet his inexorable gaze.

'Don't tempt me towards further retribution,' he warned implacably, and her lips trembled beneath his intense scrutiny.

'Will you please leave?' She swallowed the lump in her throat, aware that he watched the movement through narrowed eyes.

'We're dining out—or have you forgotten?'

Lisa lifted a hand and pushed back a swathe of hair that had fallen forward over her shoulder. 'And if I refuse to go?'

'We'll order in, and eat here.'

Lisa closed her eyes momentarily, then opened them, defeat mirrored in their depths. 'If we stay in this apartment, we'll probably end up practically *slaying* each other,' she managed wearily.

'Go and fix your face,' Rick voiced quietly, and she was halfway across the lounge when the doorbell sounded.

A further insistent peal quickened her steps, and with customary caution she depressed the intercom button.

'Who is it?'

'Dammit, Lisa—*Tony*!'

'Oh hell', she muttered indistinctly. 'Just a minute.' She glanced back over her shoulder at the invincible man standing near the window, then took a deep breath and pulled the door open. 'How did you know I was home?'

'I rang the studio.' He raked a hand through his fair wavy hair, ruffling it into attractive disorder. 'What's all this about you finishing early? I thought you said you wouldn't be home until six—at least.'

He sounded faintly accusing, and she lifted a hand in an impotent gesture, then let it fall. Where did she begin? 'I—'

'Aren't you going to perform an introduction?'

Lisa swung round to see Rick standing indolently at ease a few feet away, his expression one of lazy amusement.

Tony looked from one to the other, then demanded of her, 'Who the hell is *he*?'

There was no moment like the present. Helplessly she indicated, 'Tony Moore—Rick Andreas.'

Neither man moved, and Lisa had the peculiar sensation they were silently sizing each other up—like jungle animals in sight of prey. Yet even as the thought occurred, so did another. Victory was a foregone conclusion, and there wasn't a thing she could do about it.

Tony appeared to sense that all was not as it seemed, and he shot her an angry questioning glance. 'What's he doing here?'

'Is there any reason why I shouldn't be here?' Rick drawled in sardonic query, and Tony looked as if he was about to explode.

'Now, look here—Lisa's my girl!'

'Correction,' Rick declared silkily. 'She's mine.'

'You're wrong!' Tony's voice rose a decibel, his expression becoming faintly belligerent, and Rick's eyes hardened measurably.

'I think not.'

Tony's gaze swivelled towards Lisa. 'What the hell is going on?'

She endeavoured to swallow the lump that had lodged awkwardly in her throat. 'Everything has happened so fast,' she attempted to explain, and fell into miserable silence as Rick leaned forward and took hold of her left hand, drawing Tony's attention to the sparkling row of diamonds. She felt almost sick at the expression she glimpsed on Tony's face.

'Lisa?' He looked thunderstruck. 'My God, you were supposed to be getting engaged—to *me*!'

'We discussed it, I know,' she began unhappily, and was interrupted with a vengeance.

'We did more than discuss it!' He pushed a hand through his hair in a gesture of total incredulity. 'Look, I don't know what's come over you, but you'd better get it straight—'

'Lisa is marrying me the day after tomorrow,' Rick stated with cynical detachment.

Tony swung round to face her, and she glimpsed his obvious lack of comprehension. 'Deny it,' he demanded.

'I can't,' she stated simply, feeling utterly wretched.

'*Why?*'

Her hand lifted in silent defence, then fluttered down to her side. 'I'm sorry you had to find out this way,' she attempted placatingly, and watched his face darken with suppressed anger.

'Sure. I'm supposed to disappear, humbly accepting that you've had a sudden change of heart,' he declared with intended sarcasm. 'Thanks, Lisa—thanks very much! You sure as hell have made me look a giant-size fool!'

'I didn't mean to,' she protested. 'You have to believe that.'

He subjected her to an angry raking scrutiny. 'There's an expensive Ferrari parked downstairs. I guess it's his. Somehow I didn't think you'd sell yourself to the highest bidder, but obviously I was wrong.' He turned abruptly and moved towards the front door. 'Forgive me if I don't tender my good wishes for the happy day.' His glance seared her to the bone. 'Personally, I hope you rot in hell!' He opened the door, then slammed it behind him.

Lisa began to shake, she couldn't help it. The events of the past few hours, coupled with this latest confrontation were suddenly too much to bear.

'Drink this.'

The directive was hard and inflexible, and she didn't possess the courage to argue. The liquid was strong, and she gasped as the neat whisky hit the back of her throat.

'All of it.'

She obeyed without question, too enervated to do otherwise, and she held out the empty glass when she had finished. 'What now?' she asked hollowly.

'We go out,' said Rick, his eyes narrowing fractionally.

'I really don't think I can.' She felt ready to burst into tears, yet stoic resolve prevented their release. All she wanted to do was take a nice long shower, then fall into bed. The thought of spending a few more hours in his company, especially the eating of food, was something she would give anything to avoid.

'Staying home alone and wallowing in self-pity won't do any good,' he told her inflexibly.

What was the use of arguing? Besides, she didn't

possess the strength to do further battle. Without a word she turned and made for the bathroom, where she alternatively sluiced hot and cold water over her face, then after patting it dry, she applied moisturiser, foundation, following it with a light dusting of power. Next came eyeshadow, liner and mascara. Blusher applied high on her cheeks added essential colour.

Lisa emerged into the lounge and picked up her coat and shoulderbag. Forcing herself to meet that dark penetrating gaze, she said evenly, 'Shall we go?'

The evening wasn't exactly a success, although in retrospect she couldn't recall any specific argument—not even a difference of opinion. The restaurant Rick had chosen exuded an understated elegance that was enhanced by the attentiveness of the staff and an excellent menu. She ate the starter he ordered for her, then toyed with the main course, forking small mouthfuls at intermittent intervals, then when his plate was empty she pushed hers to one side, refused dessert and sipped her coffee while he ordered the cheese board. Throughout it all, they maintained a seemingly companionable silence interjected on occasion as Rick made some innocuous comment to which she invariably gave a monosyllabic response.

'*Rick!*' A soft feminine voice intruded with obvious delight. 'I haven't heard from you in ages!' The last query was delivered with throaty seductiveness, and Lisa turned slightly to discover if the owner matched the voice.

She did. A few inches over five feet of voluptuous femininity stood poised before them, clothed in an exclusive designer label Lisa recognised at a single glance.

'Chantal Roussos—Lisa Gray,' Rick introduced with applaudable ease, and Lisa summoned a courteous smile.

'Chantal,' she murmured politely, and received a cursory glance by return.

'Why don't you join us, darling?' Chantal entreated of Rick. 'Damon is at the bar entertaining Samantha and Alex. It would be divine if we could get together.'

'Perhaps another time,' Rick refused with a smile, and incurred a pouting moue.

'Why not now? There are a few empty tables, and it would be simple enough to arrange.'

'Doubtlessly,' he declared smoothly. 'However, Lisa and I prefer to be alone.'

'I'll ring and confirm a definite date, darling,' Chantal insisted with a trace of petulance. '*Soon*, darling,' she purred provocatively. 'I can hardly wait.'

'Good heavens!' Lisa breathed with amusement the instant Chantal Roussos was out of earshot. 'You certainly have a conquest there!'

One eyebrow slanted in open cynicism. 'You think so?'

'Oh, *darling*,' she mimicked with disgraceful mockery. 'I know so!'

Rick effected an imperceptible shrug. 'She's the daughter of a business associate.'

'How—nice!'

His dark eyes raked her expressive features, pinning her gaze. 'Precisely what do you mean?'

She afforded him a dazzling smile. 'Daughters—*sisters*, of business associates, they appear to be your speciality.'

'Don't make any implications you can't substantiate,'

Rick warned with a hint of steel, and she wondered at her own temerity in goading him.

'Did that hit a raw spot? It wasn't intentional.'

'Have some more champagne.'

'Perhaps I need it,' Lisa accepted wryly. 'Unless I'm mistaken, we're about to be invaded.'

Chantal Roussos certainly scored full marks for persistence, and to give him his due, Rick handled the situation with urbanity, completing introductions and ordering more champagne while a hovering waiter quickly moved a nearby table and chairs to accommodate Chantal and her companions.

'Well, darling,' Chantal beguiled Rick, her eyes over-bright with an eagerness Lisa found faintly sickening, 'what have you been doing with yourself lately?'

Rick leaned well back in his chair, his expression one of amused indulgence. 'I've been in the States for the past two months. I've been back only a few weeks,' he elaborated with indolent ease, and the other girl gave a provocative smile.

'So that's why I haven't seen you around. I must get Daddy to invite you to dinner. I'll ring you.'

Good grief, Lisa decided with something akin to amusement, she's practically eating him alive!

'I doubt I'll be available,' Rick declared with thoughtful deliberation.

'Another trip, darling? I'm due for holidays soon.' Her eyes were particularly eloquent as she leaned towards him—showing, Lisa observed, a more than generous cleavage as her gown parted even further. 'I had thought—Spain, perhaps. What do you think?'

'The choice is yours,' he responded urbanely, and she arched deliberately,

'Where are you off to, Rick? I don't particularly want to travel alone.'

'Then I suggest you find a companion.'

The pout was deliberate, and on the right man would have had a devastating effect. 'I had hoped you might keep me company.'

'Impossible, I'm afraid. I doubt if my wife would be enamoured of the idea,' he drawled, and Lisa held her breath, feeling as if she was part of a tableau being enacted before an audience. In a way, it was true, for Chantal's friends were viewing the proceedings with avid interest, rather like a tennis match between professionals!

'Your wife?' Chantal queried delicately, her eyes narrowing and her face becoming vaguely pinched.

His smile didn't quite reach his eyes. 'I'm thirty-four,' he offered reasonably. 'Is it so surprising that, I've now elected to enter the state of matrimony?'

'But with *whom*?' The last word appeared to rise half an octave.

Lisa felt quite sorry for the girl. She was obviously perplexed, and perhaps felt, quite fairly, that she had a stake in sharing Rick's future.

'Lisa,' he murmured, shooting her a look of such warmth it was all she could do not to reel back with surprise.

'Congratulations,' Chantal proffered magnanimously, although her eyes were positive icicles. She turned towards Lisa and summoned an over-bright smile. 'He's rather a handful, sweetie, but definitely worth the effort—*if* you can manage to hold his interest long enough!'

'I'm not at all concerned on that count, Chantal,' she

declared mildly. 'But thanks for the advice.'

'Well, this calls for a celebration. It isn't very often one of my favourite men becomes engaged,' Chantal declared in a brittle voice, and one of her companions made a slight demure, indicating that their presence was probably unpropitious, and perhaps they should relocate themselves at another table.

'Actually,' Chantal deliberated, giving Lisa a hard speculative glance, 'you look vaguely familiar. Have we met somewhere?'

'It's possible,' she agreed. 'Although I can't recall an occasion.'

'I think I've seen a picture of you in a magazine,' Samantha offered pensively. 'In fact, I'm sure I have.'

'Lisa does photographic modelling,' Rick enlightened her sardonically, and Chantal's expression became cat-like.

'Oh, *that* sort of modelling,' she purred, shooting Lisa a malevolent glance. 'Doesn't it embarrass you posing *au naturel*, as they say?'

Lisa returned the look with equanimity. 'It undoubtedly would—if I did,' she declared evenly, adding with silky smoothness, 'However, I work with Sacha Fabres. If you're familiar with fashion, you're undoubtedly aware of his reputation?'

The other girl's eyes glittered. 'Oh, sorry, darling,' she offered with saccharine sweetness, dismissing airily, 'When you mentioned photographic modelling, I naturally assumed you dabbled in its—er—' she let her voice falter deliberately, 'seamier side.'

Without undue haste, and with considerable panache, Lisa turned to her newly-acquired fiancé and placed a hand on his arm. 'Dance with me, Rick?' She put everything into making her smile appear alluring, and briefly entertained the thought that perhaps she had missed her vocation. She lifted her hand, then let it fall. 'The band is playing something romantic. It seems a pity to let it go to waste.'

His eyes gleamed with hidden humour as he stood to his feet. 'My, my,' he murmured musingly as he led her on to the dance-floor. 'I thought the sparks would fly any minute!'

'Your taste in feminine—*companions*,' she said with soft emphasis, 'leaves a lot to be desired.'

'My taste in women is impeccable,' Rick drawled. 'I have limited control, however, over those of your species who persist in clamouring for my attention.'

She spared him a look of utter enmity. 'Oh, I'm sure there's a positive *bevy* of nubile females just waiting to tear my eyes out!'

'You make me sound like a rake,' he mused, not a whit disturbed, and she could have hit him!

'I don't particularly care if you have a harem,' she told him sweetly. 'In fact, I'd welcome it.'

'One woman at a time,' he mocked. 'Anything else brings countless complications.'

'Well, count me out,' she declared vehemently, and heard his faint chuckle.

'On the contrary,' he insisted softly, 'I've just counted you *in*.' His eyes were frankly taunting as he slanted, 'Or have you forgotten?'

'I think,' Lisa announced stoically, 'I've had enough. I'd like to go home.'

'By all means.'

Back at their table he proffered a few words in excuse, and Lisa thought her face would crack with the effort of maintaining a smile as she bade Chantal Roussos and her friends goodnight.

It was almost eleven when they reached the car, and during the short drive to her apartment neither offered so much as a word by way of conversation. When the car pulled up in the courtyard she reached for the doorclasp, and slid out with the briefest of farewells, only to find as she reached the entrance foyer that Rick was behind her.

'There's no need for you to come up,' Lisa declared distantly, and Rick slanted her a wry glance.

'I'll see you safely indoors.'

The elevator doors slid open, and once inside, it transported them to the designated level with swift precision.

Unlocking her door, he solemnly handed her the key, then placed a hand on the doorjamb.

'James has arranged for Ingrid to accompany you on a shopping expedition tomorrow,' he told her, slanting a wry glance at her faint grimace. '"Something old, something new, something borrowed . . ."—isn't that how it goes?'

Her eyes met his evenly. 'I think I'll turn up in *black*,' she said hollowly.

The edges of his mouth twisted into a cynical smile. 'Not virginal white?'

The look she thrust him held bitter enmity. 'Somehow I don't think I could opt for the traditional bridal image.'

'Pity,' he drawled, and she turned away from the sudden gleam in those dark eyes.

'I'm tired,' she said quietly, and it wasn't untrue. She felt utterly weary, and longed for the solitude of her own company.

'I'll call for you tomorrow evening at seven,' Rick told her, and she drew a deep breath.

'I'd prefer not to see you until Friday.'

'Five minutes before the civil ceremony, I presume?'

'Something like that.'

Hands settled on her shoulders, forcing her round to face him, and she stood stiffly within his grasp.

'What do you want?' she queried tonelessly.

'This.'

His head lowered down to hers, and she closed her eyes in an attempt to shut out an inevitable onslaught. Instead, his touch was light and evocative, his lips brushing hers with the merest hint of sensual promise before trailing up to press closed each eyelid in turn, then she was free.

When she opened her eyes he was gone, and Lisa quietly closed and locked the apartment door, then made her way towards the bedroom.

Ingrid proved an enthusiastic companion, more than making up for Lisa's obvious lack of interest, and by the end of the day there was an assortment of parcels reposing on the rear seat of the Mazda. After the first hour, Lisa simply gave up arguing with her sister-in-law and agreed to every suggestion made. Quite what James had told his wife about his sister's forthcoming marriage, Lisa was unable to comprehend, for Ingrid referred to it as a whirlwind romance and didn't once seek to caution on the rapidity of events. Perhaps she thought the groom's considerable wealth dispensed with any self-doubts, and added an air of respectability to the entire proceedings.

'You're dining with us tonight,' Ingrid informed her as

Lisa eased the Mazda into a steady stream of traffic heading north from the city.

'I am?' Lisa queried, then muttered beneath her breath as a car on her left attempted to cross lanes and nose in ahead of her.

'Not just you, darling,' her sister-in-law chided with a faint laugh. 'Rick, too.'

Lisa pushed the brakes and jabbed the horn simultaneously. 'Male chauvinist—no patience at all, and unable to bear being behind a woman driver!' she muttered viciously, slipping the gear shift into first with unnecessary force.

'My goodness,' Ingrid commented faintly, shooting her a startled glance, 'I think the strain is beginning to get to you!'

Oh, *damn*, Lisa cursed silently. If she wasn't careful, she'd be in for all kinds of questions—most of which she'd prefer not to have to answer! 'I'm tired,' she excused with a conciliatory smile. 'And suffering from pre-wedding nerves. You know how it is.'

'Of course,' Ingrid soothed. 'You'll be glad when it's all over.'

The problem was that it was only just *beginning*! Even the mere thought of Rick assuming the role of lover made her head whirl. Not with joyful longing, as Ingrid obviously supposed—but apprehensive abhorrence! To date he hadn't shown he possessed a scrap of tenderness in his make-up, and there could be little doubt he intended consummating their union—with or without her compliance.

'I'll deposit all these packages in my apartment,' Lisa decided. 'I can pick up a change of clothes at the same time, which will save me coming back again.'

'What about Rick?' Ingrid queried.

What about him? she longed to scream. 'I'll ring and let him know,' she said, and she did—more than an hour later. Not wanting to speak with him, she simply left a message with his secretary and hung up before that epitome of efficiency could transfer the call.

Helping to supervise Simon and Melissa while Ingrid became lost in a flurry of activity in the kitchen provided an essential diversion, and Lisa willingly assisted with the children's homework before seeing them into a bath and then sitting them down at the kitchen table for their evening meal.

'Don't see why we can't eat with you and stay up late,' Simon, the elder of the two, grumbled, and incurred his mother's admonishing frown.

'I've already explained,' Ingrid declared sternly. 'Now, I don't want to hear another word. You can stay downstairs until Mr Andreas arrives, then after you've been introduced you will politely excuse yourselves and go to Simon's room where you can both watch television for an hour. If I hear one peep out of either of you, you won't be allowed to stay up late tomorrow night.'

'We're coming to your party,' Melissa announced with round eyes. 'I've got a new dress and new shoes. There's going to be a big cake, too,' she added. 'Mummy said so.'

'I've got to wear long trousers and a tie,' Simon tossed in disgust, and Lisa threw him an impish smile.

'But you'll look very handsome,' she assured him, seeing him brighten somewhat. 'I'll be so proud of you.'

'Me, too?' Melissa demanded, and Lisa leant down to give them each a hug.

'Of course. I'm going to have an early night, too. I'll need ten hours' sleep if I want to look beautiful for tomorrow.'

'I've finished,' the little girl declared, eyeing her empty plate with satisfaction before casting her brother a frowning glance. 'Hurry up, Simon. Let's go and watch from the window, then we can see when Aunty Lisa's man is coming.'

'Are your faces clean?' Ingrid asked automatically, and received a resounding affirmative. 'Off you go, then. Bless you,' she murmured as Lisa swiftly cleared the table and placed the children's plates and cutlery into the sink.

'Good heavens, what for?'

'Handling them and averting a quarrel. Simon is going through a terrible bossy stage where having a younger sister is an encumbrance not to be condoned. If she was a boy he could play any number of games with her. The fact that she tries so hard to be a tomboy just to please him only gives him all the more reason to condemn.'

'He's growing up. Give him a few more years, and he'll delight in showing her off to all his friends,' Lisa offered absently, and incurred her sister-in-law's faint grimace.

'Any homilies as to how I can survive those next few years?'

'You'll manage beautifully,' Lisa conceded, knowing it to be a fact. 'Shall I set the table?'

'Please. You know where everything is kept. I'm just about organised, thanks to modern technology and a microwave oven!'

James' arrival home received an enthusiastic greeting from his offspring, then, showered and changed, he emerged downstairs to attend to the drinks cabinet in readiness for their guest.

At precisely seven, the illumination of powerful headlights in the driveway and the excited cries of both children announced Rick's arrival, and Lisa felt the nerves in her stomach begin to tighten. By the time he entered the front door, and within seconds, the lounge, she was conscious of experiencing physical pain in that region.

His coat discarded, he looked incredibly formidable in a dark business suit, immaculately-knotted silk tie, and fine snowy linen. He acknowledged both women with a warm smile, then stood indolently at ease as both children were introduced.

'Aren't you going to kiss Aunty Lisa?' Melissa asked with disappointment and the naïveté of the very young.

'I was about to remedy that omission,' Rick intimated, and Lisa could only stand still as he crossed to her side.

A fixed smile hovered on her lips as his head lowered down to hers, and she closed her eyes against the bitter anger she felt as his mouth closed over hers in brief hard contact.

'Whisky, Rick?' James queried expansively, crossing to the well-stocked cabinet to attend to his guest's needs. 'Girls?'

'Just mineral water,' Lisa said quietly. 'I'll have wine with dinner.'

'Likewise,' Ingrid smiled, and turned to the children. 'Say goodnight. I'll be up after we've had dinner to tuck you in.'

Melissa was first, turning her small face upwards to the man who stood a good head taller than her father. 'Do I call you Uncle Rick, now you're going to marry Aunty Lisa?'

His lips widened into a slow smile. 'I'd like that.' He solemnly took Simon's outstretched hand and shook it. 'Goodnight.'

The thought of acquiring a new uncle proved a fascinating experience, and it was a further few minutes before both children took their leave.

Ingrid was an adept hostess, and she responded charmingly to Rick's proffered enquiry as to the success of their day's shopping. She more than made up for Lisa's lack of conversation, and refused any assistance when Lisa offered to help serve dinner.

The food was delectable, but it could have been sawdust for all the notice Lisa took in forking it into her mouth. Rick and James maintained sophisticated small-talk related to the sphere of business, and for the most part Lisa let it flow over the top of her head.

It was apparent that James was slightly in awe of the younger man, his manner at times decidedly deferential, and Lisa felt vaguely irritated that her brother should belittle himself to any extent.

'Are you planning on having a few days away?'

Lisa heard Ingrid's query and cast Rick a startled glance, catching his faint amusement as he responded,

'We're flying up to Townsville on Saturday. I thought we'd spend the weekend on Magnetic Island.'

She almost choked at that revelation, and reached hurriedly for her glass, taking a few reviving sips of wine. The thought of sharing days in a honeymoon existence sent her into a state of extreme nervous anxiety. The *nights* didn't bear contemplation!

Somehow she managed to get through the ensuing two

hours, pleading the need for an early night in order to escape at a reasonable hour.

'I'll drive you home.'

Lisa cast Rick a slight smile—difficult, when all she wanted to do was *hit* him. 'There's no need for you to leave yet. Besides, I have my car.'

In seeming slow motion he caught hold of her hand and lifted it to his lips, taking time to kiss each finger in turn. 'Nonsense, darling. Of course I'll take you home.' His eyes gleamed with a hidden warning, then he turned towards Ingrid and James. 'If you'll excuse us?'

'Very wise of you,' Ingrid murmured, casting Lisa an affectionate glance. 'I'll collect you around nine in the morning.'

Lisa's eyes widened fractionally, and it was all she could do not to burst into angry speech as her sister-in-law explained,

'Darling, you'll leave for the register office from here. James and I can't possibly let you *think* of anything else.' She gave a light laugh. 'And it's bad luck for you to see Rick before the ceremony.'

'I won't need all day to get ready,' Lisa demurred half-heartedly, only to have her protestation cast aside.

'Nonsense! It's simply not done for you to spend any part of your wedding day alone. You agree, don't you, Rick?' asked Ingrid, and gave a smile of satisfaction as he concurred.

'Afraid I might abscond?' Lisa demanded the instant the Ferrari cleared the driveway some five minutes later. She was consumed with frustrated rage at the way her life was being manipulated, and she hated not being in control.

'I haven't discounted the possibility,' Rick drawled enigmatically, and she rounded on him in fury.

'I'd like to,' she vented vengefully. 'My God, you can't know how much!'

'But you won't,' he stated imperturbably, shooting her a penetrating glance.

'Perhaps you'd care to explain,' she began with heavy sarcasm, 'precisely why we're embarking on a supposed "honeymoon"?'

'Because it's expected.'

'I doubt you do anything *expected*,' she said hatefully. 'Can't we just stay home?'

Rick swung the wheel with ease, then negotiated a busy intersection. 'No. The arrangements have already been made,' he informed her coolly.

'Then unmake them,' she snapped. 'I'm not going away with you.'

'Indeed you are,' he insisted silkily. 'Whether with reluctant dignity, or hoisted over my shoulder. The choice is yours.'

She reached for the door-handle, uncaring of the speed with which the car was travelling, then cursed to discover the automatic lock was in force. 'Damn you,' she muttered as angry tears clouded her vision. '*Damn you to hell!*'

She stared straight ahead in angry silence, seeing nothing of the passing traffic as the car ate up the kilometres with ease, and it seemed only scant minutes before it drew to a smooth halt outside her apartment block.

'There's no need for you to come up.' Did she utter those words? It didn't seem possible that that stiff little voice was her own.

'We've been through this before,' Rick drawled, then he slid out from behind the wheel and came round to open her door.

'Why play the gentleman? We both know it's merely a facade.' Lisa stalked ahead of him and unlocked the outer door, and once inside the foyer she crossed to the elevator and jabbed the button, entering the confined space the instant she was able.

It was useless to hope she could make it to her apartment and close the door behind her, so she didn't even try. Instead, she handed him the key and stood as he unfastened the lock.

'Goodnight.' Lisa uttered the words in a stilted voice, and her eyes were fixed in the region of his chin.

'Until tomorrow,' Rick bade sardonically, then added with soft mockery, 'Sweet dreams.'

The look she cast him would have turned a lesser man to stone, but he merely inclined his head, then moved across the corridor to summon the elevator.

CHAPTER FIVE

It not only rained all through the following day, the inclement weather provided gale-force winds which Lisa secretly thought were particularly appropriate in view of the nature of her marriage to Rick Andreas.

The ceremony at the register office was unbecomingly brief, and it seemed unbelievable that those few phrases could change the pattern of her life.

The man who was now her husband looked even more remote and indomitable, attired in an impeccably tail-ored dark business suit, looking for all the world as if he was attending a board meeting rather than being a participant at his own wedding.

Champagne flowed among the few guests standing in the formal lounge of his Vaucluse mansion—Lisa couldn't for the life of her call it *home*. In fact, cham-pagne appeared to have flowed from an unlimited supply during the past four hours, she decided a trifle wryly. Loyal servants had dispensed hors d'oeuvres, followed at seven by dinner, and now during a final toast to the health and happiness of the bride and groom.

With the utmost discretion James signalled to Ingrid and indicated their intention to leave. Lisa wanted to scream out for them to stay, but her silent pleas went unheeded, and within a matter of minutes their exit was followed by the remaining guests until there was no one left in the room except her formidable husband.

'May I have another drink?' The words tripped tritely

off her tongue, and incurred a dark probing glance.

'I think you've had sufficient,' Rick observed wryly, and she spared him a solemn assessing look from beneath long fringed lashes.

'Playing the heavy husband so soon, Rick—*darling*?'

'You ate practically nothing at dinner,' he stated dryly. 'Your concerned sister-in-law assured me that bridal nerves prevented you from doing little more than nibble less than a slice of toast for breakfast, and an apple followed by black coffee for lunch.' One eyebrow rose in slanting query. 'While I can appreciate your— apprehension, I'd prefer to have you awake and *aware* when our marriage is consummated.'

'Well, hard luck,' Lisa declared inelegantly. '*I* intend to be enveloped in an alcoholic haze.'

'Only an innocent would seek such an escape,' he mocked, and she laughed.

'Really? Do women usually fall over themselves to invite your favours?' There was a certain danger in goading him, but she was past the point of caring. Moistening her lips, she offered him a dazzling smile. 'I do hope you're good, darling. I shouldn't like to be disappointed.' She had to be mad, she thought hysteri- cally. Rick wasn't a man to suffer such bantering lightly, and to continue could only bring retribution. A sudden spasm of dizziness assailed her, and she very carefully subsided into a nearby chair, then equally carefully placed her half-empty glass down on to a glass-topped table.

'I think you'd better go to bed,' Rick drawled wryly, and she slowly shook her head.

'I can't.'

'Why not?'

She looked up at him, and he seemed suddenly to be looming far too close. 'Because if I do, you'll come, too.'

'Would that be so bad?'

His voice sounded close, and her eyes widened as she realised he had seated himself beside her. At such proximity she was aware of several things at once. Dark brown eyes agleam with wry amusement, and the faintly cynical curve of his sensuous mouth. If she wanted, she could reach out and touch him.

'I'd like some coffee,' she murmured, momentarily closing her eyes against the strange fascination that had begun to assail her senses. 'And perhaps a sandwich. Certainly no more champagne. Is it still raining? I'd like some fresh air.'

'You'd get blown away in the force of the wind,' Rick declared, standing to his feet in one easy movement. 'I'll organise something to eat from the kitchen.'

As soon as he left the room she relaxed, letting her head rest against the back of the chair. The events of the past few days and the added effect of too much champagne took their toll, and her eyelids drooped, then slowly closed.

She was dreaming, paradoxically assuming the role of a bewitched bride attired in flowing satin and tulle, and she was walking down a long aisle towards an altar which seemed to get further and further away with each step she took. She could see the backs of two men, one tall and dark-haired, the other a head shorter with fair wavy hair, and both were dressed in dark suits. She appeared to increase her step, almost hurrying in her effort to reach them, and at last she did. Her look of relief quickly turned to horror as the dark-haired man stepped forward and took her hand, and all she could think of was the need to stop the ceremony and explain that she was being married to the wrong man.

'Lisa! Wake up!'

She heard the words, and they seemed too real to be part of her dream. Her eyelids flickered open, and she found herself gazing into the face of the man whose features she had thought to be a figment of her imagination. Then it all came flooding back, and she could have cried at the futility of it all.

'Sarah has made you some sandwiches,' Rick told her, indicating a plate on a nearby table. 'And some coffee.'

Lisa accepted the cup and saucer from his hand with a muttered 'thanks', then slowly sipped the aromatic brew. It had a reviving effect, and although she didn't feel hungry, she ate two of the delectable sandwiches and finished her coffee.

'What time are we leaving in the morning?' She felt quite wide awake, and anything was worth the effort to prolong her ascent to the upper floor—and bed.

'Yannis will drive us to the airport at seven in order to catch the early flight north,' Rick informed her imperturbably, levering his lengthy frame down beside her.

Thrown into a state of confusion, she reached for another sandwich, biting into it with evident enjoyment. 'Everyone has gone. Isn't it a little early to wind up the party?'

'It's after eleven,' he said with a trace of cynical amusement. 'Our guests were being diplomatic in leaving—imagining we couldn't wait to be alone.'

'While nothing could be further from the truth,' she uttered without thought, and could have cursed her irreverent tongue.

'Another coffee?'

Lisa cast him a quick glance from beneath her heavily fringed lashes. 'Are you trying to sober me up?'

'Providing you with yet another tactic in which to delay the inevitable,' Rick said silkily, and it was all she could do not to hit him.

'Actually, I am rather tired.' She stood to her feet and turned to look down at him. 'Am I supposed to explore the upper regions of the house and blunder into the correct room, or are you going to lead the way?'

'By all means,' Rick drawled, standing to his feet. He caught hold of her arm and began walking towards the door.

She had to be mad, she decided as she ascended the stairs. A light bubbly laugh choked in her throat. It was scarcely the time to wish she had indulged in sexual pursuits. In this day and age, she was a rarity; her ideals and moral principles too old-fashioned to be believed. If she had participated, she wouldn't now be a mass of shivering nerves at the mere thought of going to bed with her husband. Her lips moved to form a wry twist. At least he *was* her husband. Perhaps if she just lay back and closed her eyes it would all be over and done with—yet even thinking about Rick as a lover was enough to make her go weak at the knees.

As they reached the top of the stairs a sudden thought erupted into speech. 'My clothes—I left a suitcase in my car.'

'Yannis brought it inside hours ago, and Sarah will undoubtedly have unpacked for you.'

'Oh,' she declared indistinctly, feeling her feet drag as Rick indicated a door to his right.

It was a spacious room, and her eyes flew of their own volition to the large bed. She felt like an animal caught in a trap from which there could be no escape, and right at that moment she didn't know whether to laugh or cry at her own foolishness for allowing herself to be caught.

'I'd like a shower.' It was a delaying tactic at best, but at least it would give her a further five, maybe ten, minutes.

'By all means,' Rick declared smoothly, indicating a door to her left. 'Your dressing-room and en-suite facilities are located here.'

'You have your own?' The question came out unbidden, and she caught his glimpse of cynical amusement.

'Relieved you don't have to share, Lisa?'

She summoned a careless shrug, then without a further word she crossed the deep-piled carpet to her dressing-room and closed the door behind her.

There was no lock evident, and a cursory inspection showed none on the bathroom door. Not that it mattered much, she decided wryly. Her devilish husband would hardly consider locks or bolts to be of any importance in his own home!

Her gaze wandered slowly over mirrored sliding doors, and intrigued, she slid them open, discovering her own clothes reposing on hangers and neatly folded into drawers. The bathroom was almost the size of an average bedroom, exquisitely tiled with an abundance of mirrors, and containing an oval marble bath complete with spa-jets, and a capacious shower stall. A marble-topped vanity unit ran the length of one wall, and there were sufficient crystal containers of varied bath essences to last for months! A carpeted floor in shades of honey was reflected in the cream marble tiles with their streaking grains, and merged with gold-plated taps. Towels in a deep shade of gold added depth and the final touch to a room that was a visual delight.

For a moment Lisa considered the spa-bath, longing for its soothing effect on her tired limbs, but opted for a shower. It was considerably less time-consuming, and if she took too long over her ablutions Rick might conceivably take it as an invitation to join her.

Even as the possibility occurred, she began discarding her clothes, then slipped beneath the stinging warmth of the projected water to complete the task in record time.

Towelled dry, her toilette completed, she moved into the dressing-room to extract nightwear from a drawer, perversely ignoring a filmy creation bought at Ingrid's insistence the previous day, and selecting instead a functional nightshirt in pink and white striped cotton that dipped to her knees and possessed a demure neckline. Her hair was quickly gathered together and braided into two long plaits. Now she was ready to face the fray!

The door swung open at a finger's touch, and Lisa took a deep steadying breath as she re-entered the bedroom. Unbidden, her gaze encompassed the room, noting the dimmed lighting, the turned-down covers on the bed, and finally the man sitting propped against the pillows.

'Well, well,' Rick drawled with indolent amusement as his dark eyes made a slow indolent appraisal. 'A few more minutes, and I would have felt bound to discover if you'd drowned!'

'I should be so lucky,' she vouchsafed with faint bitterness, her eyes averting to the subdued wall-light beyond his head. He looked totally at ease, darn him! Relaxed, even. The book he had been reading reposed on the bedcovers, and she felt her anger rise. He didn't appear a whit disturbed by what was about to take place. *God!* Why should he? She was just another female in a line of countless others who had undoubtedly gone before her.

'Are you going to stand there all night?'

Her eyes skimmed to his, and her stomach began a series of somersaults at the expanse of muscled chest above the covers. Strong sinewy shoulders bore a deep even tan, and he looked incredibly fit and virile.

'You surely don't expect me to show enthusiasm?' she countered, striving to keep her voice even. The loud thumping she could hear had to be her heart!

'It's a little late for a display of bridal jitters,' Rick opined dryly, regarding her through faintly narrowed eyes.

'You're right,' she declared hollowly, standing rooted to the spot. She couldn't move a further step forward if her life depended on it.

'You want me to come and get you?'

Even on her first modelling assignment she hadn't been this nervous! Stoically, she decided she had two choices—either slip into bed and suffer in silence, or turn and run! Her head dictated the former, but all her instincts screamed out in favour of the latter!

'Anyone would think I was about to become your executioner,' Rick drawled.

'Perhaps it would be better if you were,' she flung bleakly.

Without a word he slid from the bed, and she closed her eyes as it became apparent he wasn't wearing a stitch of clothing.

'Little fool!' he snapped roughly, catching hold of her shoulders. 'Stop playing the child!'

Her eyes flew open in anger as she lifted her chin. 'Is that what you want?' she demanded defiantly. 'I'm not a simpering siren, and I can't even pretend to like you.'

'It isn't required that you should do so,' he declared silkily, and she retaliated without thought,

'Of course not. I'm to be an object of lust, and to hell with my feelings!'

Rick's smile bore little humour. 'You're talking like a naïve schoolgirl. If you have any sense, you'll stop acting out this charade before I lose my temper.'

'I don't have any sense,' she hissed furiously. 'If I possessed even a modicum of it, I wouldn't have allowed myself to be placed in this farcical situation!' His hands tightened over her shoulders, and she winced at the pain he inflicted. 'Dammit—let go! You're hurting me!'

'You'd try the patience of a saint,' he muttered dangerously, pulling her close, ignoring her struggles with an ease that was galling.

His mouth closed over hers with brutal savagery, forcing her lips apart in a kiss that shocked her into motionless quiescence. She wanted to cry and rage at her own stupidity in goading him to an extent where he resorted to anger. If only she'd kept a rein on her temper he might have accorded her some consideration, whereas now she had unleashed violence on to her hapless head.

She felt bruised, mentally as well as physically, and when the pressure finally eased and he lifted his head she had to hold on to him for fear of falling.

Rick's eyes darkened measurably as hers widened and became locked to his, and he conducted a slow raking appraisal of her slender form. 'This is a nightgown?' he questioned, reaching out a stray finger to trace the neckline.

His voice had lowered to a seductive murmur, and was beginning to have the strangest effect on her equilibrium. When she didn't answer he placed a finger and thumb beneath her chin and lifted it high. 'Your hair,' he murmured, letting his eyes rove over her subdued features. 'Why braid it?'

'If I leave it loose, it gets into an impossible tangle.'

Slowly he untied one ribbon, then the other, undoing each plait and threading his fingers through her hair until it flowed down her shoulders in a glorious silky mass. 'That's better.'

She felt his hands at her nape, urging her head back as he lowered his own, and she was powerless to move away as his lips brushed hers with tantalising gentleness. Her eyelids slowly closed, shutting out his dark satanic features, and she became a victim of sensual seductiveness as with practised ease he sought to bring alive each and every nerve-end until her entire body seemed one pulsing ache.

Feeling as if she was floating, it wasn't until she sensed the soft warmth of the bed beneath her back that she realised where she was, and a murmur or protest escaped her lips as she strugged to sit upright. 'Don't— please!'

'You allow me to get this far, then say "don't"?' Rick queried in cynical disbelief, as she cast him a purely desperate glance.

'I never intended it to get this far.'

'There can be no going back, Lisa,' he told her hardily, pinning her to the mattress with an ease that was galling, and she lashed out in fear.

'Let me go, damn you!'

For one infinitesimal second Rick looked coldly furious, then his body trapped hers, and in a moment of blind panic she began to fight, striking him where she could, balling her fists to punch and pummel like a demented she-cat as she struggled to be free of him.

'It's a little late for histrionics,' Rick reiterated harshly, and catching first one hand and then the other he held them together above her head.

His face was close, and she could see the cold fury evident in his dark eyes. Her breathing came in ragged gasps and her breasts heaved from her recent exertion. Stupid angry tears welled and threatened to spill, and she blinked hurriedly, willing them not to fall and add to her humiliation.

'Why make it difficult for yourself?' he drawled sardonically, and she responded mulishly,

'Forgive me, but I simply can't give in to you.'

'You will,' he promised with silky detachment, and she retaliated swiftly,

'You have a giant-sized ego!'

'No. Merely a vast experience with women.'

'Of whom doubtless few have provided resistance!'

A cynical smile twisted the edges of his mouth. 'You're something of a termagant, Lisa Andreas,' he accorded softly. 'I'm tempted to make you weep, then have you beg for the release only my possession can give.'

Her eyes sparked with bitter enmity. 'Only a savage—*pagan* would do such a thing!'

'Such positive damnation,' he mocked.

'It will only succeed in making me hate you all the more,' she vented stormily, and almost died at the look of chilling implacability that carved his features into a frightening mask.

'As you are already convinced you hate me, what have I to lose?'

His mouth crushed hers, seeking a possession that demanded her total surrender, and her breath became trapped in her throat as he relentlessly sought to annihilate her very soul. Then, not content, his mouth moved to the throbbing pulse at the base of her throat before trailing lower to the soft swell of her breasts. His tongue became an erotic instrument as he alternatively teased and kissed each tender peak, and she cried out in sudden pain as he bit into the soft flesh, feeling a shaft of pleasure explode deep within as he refused to desist.

It was crazy to feel this way, and she began to whimper, pleading with him to halt the wayward path his hand was taking as it trailed ever lower, seeking and taking liberties that brought her arousal to fever pitch. Yet still he didn't stop, and she felt the hot angry tears of frustration burn her cheeks as his head moved in the path of his hand. Then she did cry out, her hands clutching hold of his head in an effort to get him to stop, and she was beyond knowing what she said as she begged, not recognising the tiny guttural sounds as her own.

Then, and only then, did he effect a bruising possession that brought a shocked scream of sudden pain, and she felt him pause, hearing his muttered oath, before his mouth covered hers, gently this time, as he coaxed her trembling lips with his own, then as the pain subsided he began to move, quietening her murmured protest until she began to sense the throbbing rhythm deep within grow of its own accord, and she caught at his shoulders in

an attempt to hold on to something tangible as the
swelling pulsating sensation exploded into myriad
quivering sensual waves that seemed to rock her entire
body.

She must have slept, for when she woke it was dark,
and for one blissful moment she thought she was in bed,
alone in her own apartment, and that the slow periphery
of a dreamlike vision was just that—a dream.

Except there was a heavy arm across her waist, holding her close to a warm muscular chest, and even as
realisation dawned, he stirred, tightening his grasp as
she attempted to move away.

'Please—I—I want to go to the bathroom,' she whispered shakily, hoping the excuse would gain her release.

She felt his breath stir the hair at her temple, then his
arm lifted and snapped on the bedside lamp.

The illumination threw her into immediate confusion
as she hastened to pull up the covers. Where was her
nightshirt? A slow painful blush crept into her cheeks as
she met Rick's dark gleaming gaze.

'I can manage to find my way in the dark,' she said
with increasing nervousness as she glimpsed the deep
lambent warmth evident in his eyes.

'Little goose,' he mocked. 'You could stumble, or
bang into the wall.'

That would be preferable to having him watch
her walk naked across the room. 'At least have the
decency—'

'Not to look?' He lifted a hand and trailed his fingers
down her nose, then moved to outline her jaw before
tilting her chin towards him. 'Would it be so terrible if I
watched my wife cross a room without any adornment?'
A slow smile curved his lips as her lashes fluttered down

over her eyes. 'You'll gradually lose such inhibitions—given time.'

'I doubt it,' she choked, then gasped as his mouth brushed hers.

'Run away, Lisa,' he bade easily. 'I promise not to look—this time.'

Feeling acutely embarrassed, she slid out of bed and made her way to the bathroom, closing the door behind her with a sigh of relief. He was an arrogant devil, and far too worldly-wise for her peace of mind. A warm tide of colour washed over her body at the thought of his sexual expertise—something she would never become accustomed to in a lifetime!

With an angry gesture she moved across to the spa-bath and turned on the taps, then flicked the switch operating the jets. The bubbling water soothed her aching limbs, and she secured her hair on top of her head, then leaned back and closed her eyes as she strove to put the past few hours out of her mind.

How long she stayed there, she had no idea, and she almost screamed when a slight movement caught the corner of her eye.

'Are you intending to stay here all night?' Rick drawled from the doorway. With a towel hitched about his hips he looked intensely virile.

'I was just about to get out,' she asserted resentfully, and watched with alarm as he calmly reached for a towel and held it in readiness. 'I'd appreciate some degree of privacy,' she muttered, forcing herself to meet his gaze—difficult, in the circumstances!

'Unless you want me to join you there, I advise you to get out—now,' he slanted, and she retaliated in defiance,

'Can't you use your own bathroom?' Her eyes deepened with anger as they swept his muscular frame. 'Or is this a further attempt to embarrass me?'

'We're man and wife, Lisa,' he declared hardily. 'And as your husband, I refuse to be denied entry to your bathroom—or anywhere else.'

Her eyes flashed with brilliant fury, then she veiled her anger by fixing her gaze at the foot of the oval bath. 'In that case, you won't object if I wander in some time while you're having a shower?' Her attempt at sarcasm failed dismally as he gave a deep husky chuckle.

'Undoubtedly I'll persuade you to share it!'

Without thought she picked up the sponge and hurled it in his direction, deriving some degree of satisfaction as it landed on his chest.

'So you want to play,' Rick drawled ruminatively, moving forward with menacing speed.

'Don't you *dare*!'

The next instant she was plucked from the bath to stand before him, one arm instinctively moving to cover her breasts while she used the other to push against his chest.

'You fiend!' she cried out, and blind anger was responsible for the fists she lashed against his shoulders, his chest, before aiming for his arrogant jaw.

His husky string of epithets was barely discernible as he sought to counter her attack, and with appalling ease he caught each of her hands and held them. 'Will you never learn?'

'Oh—go to hell!'

For a moment she thought he meant to strike her, then he hauled her close and his mouth fastened on hers with bruising punishing force. If he meant to teach her a lesson, he succeeded, for in those timeless minutes she prayed for merciful oblivion and it became apparent that her request went unanswered as he pillaged her tender mouth, ignoring her moan of despair, until with a gesture of disgust he thrust her at arms' length.

Eyes impossibly blurred with unshed tears failed to glimpse the smouldering bleakness in his own as he raked her expressive features and saw the evidence of his diabolical devastation.

His narrowed gaze took in the faint bruising on her body, the marks of his passion, and with a muttered oath he caught up a towel and wrapped it round her slim form. With strangely gentle movements he dried the moisture from her skin, then moved to her dressing-room and deftly extracted a nightgown and slipped it over her head.

Lisa was unable to look at him, and she kept her eyelids resolutely lowered as she suffered his ministrations. She felt completely drained, and didn't have the will to resist when he caught her into his arms and carried her through to the bedroom. Releasing her down on to the bed, he pulled up the covers, then moved round to slide in beside her.

For several minutes she lay tense with fear that he might reach for her, then exhaustion slowly took its toll and she slipped into deep dreamless somnolence, unaware and uncaring of the man lying within touching distance beside her.

CHAPTER SIX

THE North Queensland tropical heat warmed her skin as Lisa stepped on to the tarmac at Townsville the following afternoon, and she suffered Rick's firm clasp of her elbow as he led the way towards the airport lounge.

With considerable ease he collected both lightweight overnight bags and enlisted the services of a taxi to transport them to their hotel.

Modern concrete and steel structures vied with older wooden buildings, some of which paint had bleached the bare wood to a silky sheen. In the residential areas gardens abounded in a blaze of rioting colour with shrubbery and climbing trailing vines. Lush vegetation proved a visual delight, and Lisa noted the cabbage trees, the pandanus palms that graced and lined the wide streets.

The hotel was a modern edifice not far from the centre of town, and after checking in Rick suggested they go down to the lounge for a drink.

'You go,' Lisa declared. 'I think I'll have a shower and rest for an hour.'

He crossed to her side and took hold of her chin, lifting it high so that she had to look at him. 'You look all eyes,' he told her, brushing his fingers against the dark circles bruising the delicate hollows.

'I didn't get much sleep last night.' She hadn't meant it to come out like that, and a light pink tinged her cheeks, making her unaccountably cross.

'Neither you did,' he acknowledged with musing cynicism. 'Have your rest, by all means. I'll be back in an hour or so.'

The relief of being alone was almost too much for her, and when he had gone she moved into the bathroom, took a long leisurely shower, then slipped into a silky wrap and lay down on the bed.

It was blissful to be free of Rick's dynamic presence, and she closed her eyes against his image, willing sleep to ease the deep aching sensation in the region of her heart.

She wanted to curse James and his business misman-agement, the economic climate which had precipitated the downhill slide, and most of all, she wanted to damn the arrogant devilish man who had taken advantage of the situation to force her into marriage.

Five years. How in the name of heaven was she going to survive five *years*? Barely twenty-four hours had passed, and already she was a nervous wreck, physically and mentally drained by an initiation into the realms of physical lust. And Rick had made no secret of the fact that he would take her again and again, wherever and whenever he pleased. It was there in his eyes, the sensual curve of his mouth.

And what if, at the end of those five years, he allowed her to go free? Could she ever face another man, live with him—*love* him? Despite her innocent naïveté, in-stinct foretold that Rick Andreas would be a hard act for any man to follow.

She slipped into sleep, and woke to find the room in darkness. The air had cooled, and there was a slight breeze wafting the curtains that hung beside the wide screened windows. A glance at her watch revealed it to be well after seven, and she stirred, swinging her legs over the edge of the bed as she reached for the light switch.

A faint gasp rushed from her lips as she saw Rick's lengthy frame reposing in a nearby chair, and she met his faint amusement with indignation.

'How long have you been there?'

'More than an hour. It seemed a pity to disturb you.'

Lisa swallowed quickly, averting her gaze from the latent sensuality in his studied glance. 'Is it too late to go down to the dining room?'

His dark eyes gleamed with faint amusement. 'We could always ring for room service.'

That held connotations of a kind she would prefer to avoid. 'Perhaps we could go for a walk and discover a restaurant,' she suggested, moving across to unfasten her overnight bag. The clothes she had packed were of the easy-care uncrushable variety, and she extracted fresh underwear and a slim-fitting sleeveless dress that was split almost to mid-thigh, gathered at the waist to afford a blouson effect, and had a deep vee front and back. With high-heeled strappy sandals it would afford a casual elegance.

'Afraid of sharing a candlelit dinner for two in this suite?' Rick mocked, watching as she crossed to the bathroom. 'Where are you going?' he demanded softly, and she answered cursorily,

'To get dressed.'

'Still so shy—after last night?'

Lisa turned on him angrily. 'Is that one of your turn-ons—watching a woman dress?' Her eyes sparked liquid fire. 'Sorry, but I'm not about to oblige!'

'Lisa,' he drawled implacably, 'I warn you—'

'And I'm warning *you*,' she berated seriously. 'I won't

be subjected to chauvinistic tyranny, just for the hell of it! You may consider you have rights, but then so do I. I'm not an unreasonable person, but I can't—*won't*, accept that I have to accede to your every whim.' She took a deep steadying breath. 'Now, if you'll excuse me, I'll go and change.'

It was a hollow victory, and didn't count for much, she decided wearily as she quickly discarded her robe and slipped into her clothes. Hair and make-up complete, she emerged into the bedroom to see his tall frame silhouetted against the window.

He turned as she reached the middle of the room, and his expression was deliberately inscrutable. 'I've booked a table at a restaurant a few blocks away. If you're ready, we'll leave.'

The food was superb, although she only picked at each course and forwent dessert entirely, electing to choose a selection from the cheeseboard, which she followed with strong black coffee.

'Would you care to dance?'

Lisa looked across the table and met his dark gaze, and was unable to discern anything other than polite uninterest. It was better than trying to cull some conversational gambit, and infinitely wiser than electing to return to their hotel room. Effecting a light shrug, she acquiesced and stood to her feet, allowing him to lead her on to the small circular dance floor.

His clasp was light yet firm, and she was aware of a strange inexplicable melting that made her ache for closer contact. Her pulse quickened as sensation ran like quicksilver through her veins, and she had to school herself against an increasing awareness that threatened to overpower her emotions. It was madness, surely a temporary insanity. She hated him, everything about him, all that he stood for. How was it possible to be swayed to any extent, when every ounce of logic demanded otherwise?

'You're very quiet,' Rick observed with faint mockery, and she lifted her face to regard him through thickly fringed lashes.

'I didn't realise you required polite conversation,' she returned evenly. 'If you'll name a subject, I'll endeavour to contribute as much as my limited knowledge permits.'

'The peace was almost too good to be true,' he slanted musingly. 'Perhaps we should opt for a silent truce?'

'Silence, yes. But a truce?' she arched wryly. 'I doubt it would last for long.'

'You're determined to dislike me?'

'How can you ever doubt it?' Lisa countered, and glimpsed the brilliance in his eyes, sensed the latent passion, and was suddenly afraid—yet strangely excited as well. It was a puzzling mixture, and she was totally perplexed, at odds to know how to deal with it.

'Shall we go back to the hotel?' His voice was a sardonic murmur and held a certain wry cynicism, almost as if he recognised the contrary pull on her emotions.

She gave a slight shrug, then let her shoulders droop. 'If that's what you want.'

'Suppose you tell me what *you* want?'

Rick had adopted the role of seducer, with devastating effect, and she determined the only way to cope with it was with light amusement.

Deliberately she let her gaze rest on his broad-chiselled features. 'Will you indulge me, Rick? Or are you merely showing condescension?'

'Try me.'

Her head tilted slightly as she pondered in consideration. 'A walk along the beach—barefoot, with the sand beneath my feet, the tide eddying at my toes, and a breeze lifting my hair.' She gave a slight smile. 'Is that too much to ask?'

His ebony-dark eyes gleamed as an answering smile tugged the edges of his lips. 'You can't believe I'll let you go alone?' he queried dryly.

She looked at his impeccably-cut jacket, the perfectly creased trousers and the hand-stitched shoes. 'You're not serious?'

An eyebrow quirked in open mockery. 'You doubt me?'

'Somehow you don't strike me as the type to throw convention to the winds.'

He looked faintly amused. 'May I venture that you hardly know me at all.'

'Don't remind me,' she said bleakly, and felt his arms tighten momentarily, then he released her and led the way back to their table.

Signalling for the bill, he extracted notes in payment, then caught hold of her hand, inexorably making for the exit.

'Where are we going?'

'To walk along the beach,' Rick drawled as they reached the street, and he slanted her a dark probing look. 'Have you changed your mind?'

She shook her head. 'No.'

There were several people about, and as they walked more than a few turned their heads for a second glance at the slim, beautiful young woman and her tall, arresting companion.

After some ten minutes they crossed the street to the park, and Lisa slipped off her high-heeled sandals, hooking the ankle straps over her fingers as she walked barefoot along the grass verge.

'No immediately accessible sandy beach, I'm afraid,' Rick told her. 'Possibly it can be reached further on, but all we have here is a retaining wall.'

'It doesn't matter,' she dismissed lightly.

'You're a contrary creature,' he murmured, draping an arm about her shoulders, and she looked out over the dark sea, skimming its surface towards the horizon.

'Why?'

'Dismissing the bright lights for the simpler pleasures.'

'Because I don't live up to the expected image most people have of a model?' she queried solemnly. 'I assure you we're quite human.'

'I don't think that can be in question,' he managed dryly, and she stopped walking, feeling stung by his cynicism.

'Let's go back.' Suddenly she was tired of this unusual camaraderie, feeling as if she was skating on thin ice and hardly daring to break the surface in case she might be plunged into liking him. It was far safer to maintain a feeling of resentful antipathy. Anything else was sheer madness.

'You haven't passed comment on the night sky,' Rick mused lazily, and reaching out he placed a hand beneath her chin and tilted it. 'It resembles diamond-studded obsidian velvet, vast and nebulous.'

'Very poetical,' she said dryly, becoming all too aware of the magic whispering over her body like a mystical nimbus. Alone with him like this, she could almost believe some elemental force was responsible for the way she felt, rendering her helpless against its irresistible pull.

Almost of its own volition her face lifted to his, and her lips parted with a soundless sigh as his mouth fastened on hers in a kiss that reduced her to a weak-willed melting supplicant. It was the first gentleness he had cared to bestow, and it was like drowning in a pool of exquisite sensation.

When he lifted his head, she stood in a bewildered daze, too enervated to move.

'Shall we go back?'

The sound of his voice brought a semblance of normalcy, and she made no demur as he draped an arm across her shoulder and began leading the way to the street.

As she reached the footpath she paused to slip on her sandals, then together they walked slowly back to the hotel.

In their suite Rick crossed to the small well-stocked refrigerator. 'Would you like a drink?'

'Something long and cool,' Lisa decided. 'Is there any fruit juice?'

'Spiked with champagne?'

'Do we have some?' she asked with mild surprise, and caught his faint amusement.

'Indeed. Shall I mix you a Mimosa?'

'Why not?' she countered lightly, moving to switch on the television. A distraction of some kind was needed, for there was a distinct danger in appearing quiescent.

Rick crossed the room and handed her a glass. 'Here's to us,' he murmured, and she sipped the contents slowly, keeping her eyes lowered as she felt his gaze roam indolently over her expressive features.

'What time does the launch leave in the morning?' She had to say *something*. The silence was playing havoc with her nervous system, and an attempt at polite conversation had never proved more difficult.

'At ten, I believe.'

'How long will we be there?'

'Two days,' he told her. 'I have to be in Melbourne on Tuesday.'

Lisa watched with idle fascination as he lifted his glass and took a generous swallow, then managed to hold his gaze as he viewed her with mocking cynicism.

'You'll gain a reprieve,' he drawled. 'Surely that's something to look forward to?'

'Definitely,' she acceded tritely. 'How long will you be away?'

'A few days—four at the most.' His eyes gleamed darkly with amusement. 'Of course, you could accompany me.'

'No, thank you,' she said sweetly. 'I'd much prefer you went alone.'

One eyebrow slanted mockingly. 'Not even if I enticed you with a luxurious suite at the Crest hotel, and prepared to indulge you a shopping spree while I'm enmeshed with business?'

Lisa shook her head. 'Sorry, it wouldn't interest me.'

'Ah,' he mused speculatively. 'It isn't the *days* you're afraid of, hmn?'

'I'm not afraid of anything,' Lisa declared evenly. 'I don't happen to like you, that's all, and the less time I'm forced to spend in your company, the better I'll be pleased.'

'Is that so?' he drawled sardonically, placing his glass down on to a nearby table. He moved towards her with deliberate indolence. 'You didn't exactly hate me last night.'

'You're an expert in the art of seduction,' she pointed out civilly, forcing herself to meet those dark cynical eyes. 'With sufficient expertise and prowess to satiate the senses. It doesn't mean I like *you*—or even myself,' she added wryly.

'Poor little girl,' he murmured. 'So logical over something that's totally beyond your control.'

'It won't happen again,' she vowed solemnly, and incurred his twisted smile.

'You think not?'

'I don't imagine you'll enjoy having a block of ice in your arms,' she ventured, attempting to step away, only to be pulled close against him with appalling ease.

'We'll see, shall we?'

She twisted her head in an effort to evade his descending mouth, then cried out as his fingers slid heedlessly through the heavy swathe of hair at her nape, tugging her tender scalp. His mouth closed over hers with unerring accuracy, forcibly branding his possession as his hands moulded her slender curves close to the hard contours of his body.

Lisa tried to resist, but the increasing pressure brought an aching warmth coursing through her veins, destroying all sensibility as passion stirred into pulsating life, and she was helpless to demur as he slowly divested her of every last item of her clothing, then began on his own.

Her breasts throbbed and burgeoned beneath the erotic treatment they received, and she became mindless, lost in a swirling sea of sensation where the only solid entity was the man himself, and she clung to him unashamedly, delighting in the wicked ecstasy of his touch as he led her to the peak of sensual fulfilment.

It was the silky feel of the sheets beneath her body that sent alarm signals spiralling to her brain, and the reality of what was about to occur suddenly brought revulsion. Dear God, how could she succumb like this? 'Let me go!' she groaned, struggling to be free of him, then gasped as he caught her hands in a painful grip.

'You expect me to stop—*now*?' Rick growled emotively, his eyes dark and slumbrous with passion as he leaned over her.

'It's—disgusting,' she whispered shakily. Her breathing was ragged, her eyes wide and luminous as she stared up at him. 'I hate you—*hate* you, for what you're doing to me!' She was filled with loathing—and outrage. At that precise moment she could have hit him, and would have, if he wasn't holding her hands. 'Let me *go*, damn you!' She twisted and turned to no avail, becoming flushed with anger and exertion until sheer fury exulted, and without thought to the consequences she sank her teeth into the sinewy muscle of his arm.

His husky imprecation rang in her ears, then she screamed as he caught the soft flesh beneath one roseate peak between his teeth in direct retaliations making her whimper and plead until at last his mouth moved to cover hers, bruising the delicate tissue as he exacted punishment. It didn't stop there, for with galling ease one powerful leg forced her thighs apart, and his subsequent actions spared her little mercy as he subjected her to the ultimate humiliation.

It seemed forever before he thrust himself away, and

she lay still, too emotionally and physically drained to move. Her eyes stared sightlessly up at the ceiling, and she didn't even blink as he pulled up the covers and switched off the light.

She wanted to cry, but no tears would come. Nothing, *nothing* could be worse than this—this total violation of body and soul.

There weren't sufficient words to describe such brutal savagery, and she was too enervated to even try. One day—even if it was months—*years*, from now, she would elicit revenge. It was a promise she intended to keep, although precisely *how* was something she would work on.

'Go to sleep,' Rick bade sardonically, and, incensed, she rolled on to her side, then cried out as two hands brought her back to face him. 'Don't turn your back on me, Lisa,' he warned implacably.

'I always sleep on my side,' she hissed, hating him with a fervour that was frightening.

'Then we'll change positions so that you sleep facing me.' With effortless ease he lifted her across his body to the other side of the bed.

'You diabolical, sadistic *bastard*!' Lisa muttered, and angry tears filled her eyes. 'Haven't you done enough?'

'Be assured I could do much worse,' Rick drawled silkily, and she responded tonelessly,

'I don't believe it.'

'Then I'd advise you not to goad me further and place yourself in the position of finding out.'

She was incapable of uttering a further word, and in the darkness the tears spilled to run slowly down her cheeks. Sleep never seemed more distant, but sheer weariness took its toll and at last she drifted into an uneasy slumber where shadowy figures lurked and emerged from their peripheral realm to haunt and taunt her, and she moved restlessly in an attempt to be free of them, seeking and finding a solid entity whose soothing voice calmed and quietened, dispensing the nightmare with blissful ease.

One of the larger islands comprising the Great Barrier Reef, Magnetic Island had been completely rebuilt after suffering the devastating effect of a tropical cyclone several years previously.

Housing a pineapple plantation, there was a lush growth of banana trees, mangoes and paw-paw, and the numerous sandy bays fringing the foreshore were a source of visual delight.

Rick ensured that they saw all the tourist attractions, but Lisa found it difficult to summon more than a desultory interest in the beauty of her surroundings.

She endeavoured to relax beneath the warmth of the sun's rays as they alternately sunbathed or swam in the hotel pool, but it seemed as if she had become an automaton, and on more than one occasion she caught the thoughtful deliberation in his gaze as it rested on her lissom form.

Subdued, she became caught up in an enveloping web of introspection, so that she appeared amenable, hardly caring about a thing except the necessity to suffer as little as possible beneath his devilish hands.

It was a relief when the two days had passed and they returned to Townsville, and, within the space of an hour, were transported to the airport.

CHAPTER SEVEN

THE clouds converged in an angry grey sky, and rain lashed the plane as it prepared to land at Sydney airport.

Yannis was already waiting in the airport lounge, and with the ease of long practice he collected their overnight bags and led the way out to the waiting car.

After the warm sunshine of the north, Lisa felt the cold wind bite right through to her skin, and she clutched the edges of her coat, pulling them together against the winter elements.

Rick followed her into the rear seat of the car, folding his length beside her, and she sat well back against the superb upholstery and pretended an interest in the passing scenery as Yannis eased his way through the traffic.

'How is Sarah?' she voiced the polite query, and received a wide smile via the rear-vision mirror.

'Fine, thank you. Terrible weather, isn't it?' he offered conversationally. 'We had high winds all through yesterday, and the rain began early this morning.'

'Any messages, Yannis?' Rick's voice was an amused drawl, and it was all she could do not to throw him an icy glare. Instead she had to be content with silence.

'A few, but nothing of any importance. They're on your desk,' the older man responded.

Lisa felt a sense of relief as they reached Rose Bay and ascended the curving hillside into Vaucluse. Within minutes they would arrive at the beautiful brick mansion. Then she could escape, for doubtless Rick would closet himself in his study, after which with a bit of luck he would drive into the city and attend to business affairs. She would have the rest of the day to herself. A number of ideas ran through her brain. She would ring James, then Ingrid, and suggest they meet for lunch. It was only three days since she had seen them, but so much had happened that it seemed forever. Suddenly the thought of how she was expected to fill her time began to assume disturbing proportion. After pursuing a career for several years and leading a reasonably active social life, she felt the emptiness yawn in front of her like a huge vacuum.

Yannis brought the large Mercedes to a halt beneath the columned portico, and almost immediately the front door opened to reveal a smiling Sarah standing in its aperture.

After the initial greeting Lisa moved towards the staircase and suffered Rick's arm about her waist until they were on the upper floor and safely into their bedroom suite.

'You can dispense with the "loving husband" charade,' she declared evenly, sparing him an icy glare, and was incensed to discover an amused gleam in the depths of those dark eyes.

'I have to be at the office by midday,' he told her with a touch of irony. 'Doubtless you'll enjoy my absence?'

'Of course,' she responded at once. 'I'll explore this vast house, telephone my brother and sister-in-law—possibly even meet Ingrid for lunch if she can manage it.' She looked up at him unwaveringly. 'Do I need to instruct Sarah as to dinner arrangements?'

'Consult with Sarah, by all means,' he answered smoothly. 'However, as there will only be the two of us, it isn't necessary.' A faint frown creased his brow. 'If you intend going into the city, you may as well ride in with me. Yannis will collect you whenever you are ready.'

Her eyes widened fractionally. 'Oh, don't be ridiculous! I have my own car, remember?'

'You're adept at starting an argument,' he drawled, and she flashed,

'Just as you're adept at finishing them!'

'Perhaps you'd be advised to remember that.'

'For heaven's sake,' she exploded, 'I'm not a child!'

'Lisa,' he warned implacably, his eyes darkening with inimical temper, 'I grow weary of these constant clashes. So far I've shown remarkable restraint. Don't push me too far.'

Her eyes flashed molten fire as she turned on him. 'What about *me*? It's a case of the old double standard, isn't it?' she demanded bitterly. 'You can exert brute force, subject me to all kinds of indignities, attempt to coerce me to obey your every whim, yet if I so much as demur, let alone retaliate, I'm relegated to behaving like a *child*. If that isn't male chauvinism at its very worst, then—'

'Shut up,' he muttered, pulling her close, and she was unable to utter another word as his mouth closed over hers with deep evocative possession that rendered her limbs boneless.

When he released her she stood in subdued silence, unable to voice a protest as he brushed his fingers down her cheek. 'This appears to be the only sphere in which we relate,' he mused idly as he tilted her chin. His eyes hardened slightly as he caught sight of her faintly swollen lips, and he bent to caress them, his touch oddly gentle. 'I must go,' he declared with regret. 'Fill the day however you please. I'll be home around six.'

Lisa watched him leave, and as soon as the door closed behind him she crossed to the telephone and rang James.

'You're back,' he concluded unnecessarily, for obviously she was—otherwise she wouldn't be ringing! 'Er—how are things?'

'What a loaded remark,' she declared wryly. 'Do you really want to know?'

'I'm concerned about your welfare,' James said heavily, and she gave him a rueful grimace.

'It's a little late for that.'

'Andreas isn't mistreating you, surely?' her brother queried scandalously, and she closed her eyes momentarily in an effort to gain some control.

'What gives you that idea?'

There followed a measurable silence. 'I'm aware that you were placed in an intolerable situation,' he said at last. 'It doesn't mean I liked putting you in that position. I'm inordinately fond of you.'

'Yes, I know.' There didn't seem any point in pursuing the subject. Besides, it was a *fait accompli*, and something she had to live with. 'I rang to see if you'll have lunch with me,' she said, deliberately keeping her voice light. 'Or are you too busy to see your only sister?'

'How about tomorrow?' he hazarded. 'I have a business lunch scheduled for today. Something I can't get out of.'

'All right,' she conceded. 'Tomorrow. What time and where?'

He named a restaurant not far from his office, and

after she had replaced the receiver, she lifted it and dialled again.

'Ingrid? How about meeting me for lunch?'

'Oh, *Lisa*!' Her voice was a distracted wail. 'Darling, I simply can't today. Simon is home with a virus, and he really can't be left.'

It appeared her luck was out. 'It doesn't matter. One day next week, perhaps?'

'I'd love to,' Ingrid enthused. 'How did the weekend go?'

Dear heaven! How did she answer that? 'Fine,' she responded evenly, and heard her sister-in-law's faint laugh.

'Oh, Lisa, you sound very reserved! However, I understand. One's sexual exploits aren't something for general discussion.'

'Give Simon my love,' Lisa instructed, refusing to be drawn. 'And ring me when you can make it for lunch.'

Damn! Now what could she do? She stood to her feet and restlessly paced the room. The number of friends she could ring at this hour of the day was few, and she hesitated over calling. She could fill in an hour with Sarah, but what about the remainder of the afternoon? Suddenly she made up her mind. There was only one thing for it—she'd drive into Double Bay and indulge herself with a shopping spree. Her bank account could stand a substantial withdrawal, and besides, Rick would discover that having a wife could prove expensive! Darn it, she had every right to spend some of his money!

Her Mazda RX7 stood in the garage, and she refused Yannis' offer to drive her in the Mercedes. Rick, it appeared, had chosen to take the Ferrari.

It seemed an age since she had driven her own car, and she eased it through the heavy wrought-iron gates, then sent it purring towards New South Head Road, and reached the exclusive suburb some ten minutes later. Parking posed little problem, and locking the car she set out with a brisk pace.

The afternoon passed swiftly as she added to her purchases without any compunction as to cost, and it was as she unloaded the last armful into the rear of her car that she was accosted by a familiar voice.

'Lisa! I've been hoping to see you.'

She stood upright and turned to see Tony standing less than a foot distant. 'Tony,' she acknowledged cautiously. 'What are you doing here?'

'I live in the area,' he said dryly. 'Or have you forgotten?'

'Of course. You startled me.' She sounded polite, and he gave a wry grimace.

'I was pretty upset the other night,' he excused. 'You knocked me for six.'

'I'm just on my way home,' she told him evenly, and he gave a rueful smile.

'Not even time to have a drink with an old friend?'

'Do you think that's wise?'

'Ten minutes', he pleaded. 'Just to prove there's no hard feelings?'

'And what do we discuss?' Lisa arched with veiled sarcasm. 'The weather?'

'You could tell me if you're happy.' He raised both hands in a gesture of defence as she opened her mouth to remonstrate. 'Okay, okay. We'll discuss the weather—anything. Just ten minutes, then I promise we'll each go our own way.'

'I'm due home in five minutes, and it's a ten-minute drive.'

He sensed her weakening, and pushed home to victory. 'Oh, come on! Surely that domineering husband of yours can allow you a ten-minute lapse? You could always say you were held up in traffic.'

'Oh, all right,' she capitulated, pushing the key into the lock and turning it. 'But only ten minutes.'

They walked half a block and entered a small exclusive bar. It was well patronised, and Tony found a vacant table near the rear.

'What will you have?'

'Lime and soda water,' Lisa decided, daring him to demur, and with a shrug he made his way towards the bar.

He was back in a few minutes with two glasses, and sat down in the opposite chair. 'Here's to life,' he murmured, raising his glass in a mocking toast.

She sipped the contents slowly, letting her eyes wander around the room. A dark head near the end of the bar seemed incredibly familiar, and as he turned she almost died with shock. *Rick!* Of all the people she would choose to run into, he would have to be the last. If he saw her, how could she attempt to brazen it out?

Almost as if he sensed her presence, he swung round and she met the coolness of his gaze, saw the faint narrowing of his eyes as he caught sight of her companion.

With mesmerised fascination she saw him murmur something to the man beside him, then he began easing his way towards her.

'Oh, *hell*!' Tony's muttered oath held an edge of fear, and not waiting for a confrontation he stood to his feet and left with an abruptness that brought a wry smile to her lips.

'Enjoying your drink?'

Lisa looked up and met his gaze fearlessly. 'Yes. Are you?'

His expression was an inscrutable mask. 'I had some unfinished business to discuss with a colleague. We decided to wind it up over a drink.'

She lifted her glass and took a generous sip, then placed it carefully down on to the table. 'He's still waiting for you.'

'Perhaps you'd care to explain what you're doing here?'

The silkiness of his voice sent shivers of apprehension slithering down the length of her spine. 'Is there a law that says I can't enjoy a drink with a friend?'

One eyebrow rose in silent query. 'He happens to be more than a friend.'

'Oh, for heaven's sake!' Lisa expostulated. 'Don't start playing the heavy husband!'

'Did you arrange to meet here?'

Her eyes flashed with brilliant anger. 'No, we didn't. Not that I expect you to believe me.'

'It's a little too much of a coincidence, wouldn't you agree?'

'Look,' she began evenly, just barely holding on to her temper. 'I've spent the afternoon shopping. Check the car if you don't believe me.' She swept him a glance of bitter enmity. 'I've been here, with Tony, less than five minutes.'

'So you say.'

That was the very limit, and she stood to her feet in one angry movement. 'I'm not staying here to be subjected to an inquisition. Go back to your—associate. I'm going home.' Her eyes sparked brilliant fire as she swept him from head to foot and back again. 'My *apartment*,' she stressed, and attempted to move past him, only to come to an abrupt halt as he caught her arm in a bruising grip.

'Come and join us,' Rick instructed grimly. 'Then we will leave—together.'

'The hell I will!'

'Lisa!' His voice held dangerous warning, which she refused to heed.

'I'm going, Rick,' she vented determinedly. 'If you try to stop me, I promise I'll cause a scene!'

'You're being exceedingly childish.'

'Am I?' she demanded wryly, and his eyes became dark flints of fury.

'We'll continue this at home,' he insisted coldly.

'Will you let me go?' Lisa demanded wearily, attempting to wrest free of his grasp.

'When I have your word that you'll drive straight home—our home,' he stressed forcefully, and she shook her head in silent refusal.

'I don't think I could bear to be near you,' she declared shakily, hating him for insinuating something that had no substance whatever.

'In that case, you will wait and I'll drive you.'

She took one look at his hawkish profile and willed herself to remain calm. Difficult, when all she wanted to do was *hit* him, and goaded much further, she surely would! 'Go to hell, Rick,' she said quietly. 'I'm no longer afraid of anything you might do.'

She almost died at the icy anger evident in those taut features, yet something was urging her on, some devilish

imp rode her shoulder, daring and defiant. It was madness, and doubtless she would be sorry afterwards, but
right at this moment she was recklessly uncaring. Without thought she threw the contents of her glass into his
face.

'Give me your car keys,' Rick insisted implacably.

Her chin tilted slightly. 'I haven't been drinking anything alcoholic,' she assured him, and almost gasped as
his grip tightened painfully. 'You're hurting me!'

'Right at this precise moment, I'd like to *thrash* you,'
he declared pitilessly.

'No doubt you will, given time,' she snapped waspishly. A sudden twist and she was free, and without
pausing she turned and fled, almost running in her haste
to escape.

She heard him behind her, and pushed her way
through the throng of patrons to the door, then began to
sprint across the pavement as fast as her high heels
would allow.

The Mazda was parked on the opposite side of the
road, and she spared a cursory glance to determine any
oncoming traffic, then stepped out on to the road. It had
begun to rain and she lowered her head in an attempt to
ward off the driving force of it.

Suddenly there was a blare of lights, accompanied
simultaneously by a hornblast and the horrendous
screeching sound of frantically applied brakes—then
nothing.

There were voices, brisk competent snatches of conversation that faded and recurred with disjointed irregu-
larity as Lisa slipped in and out of an inky black void.
Her body felt strangely weightless, yet filled with a dull

aching pain, and she kept her eyes closed in an effort to avoid a return to reality. Insignificant segments floated in kaleidoscopic confusion through her brain, until like a jigsaw the pieces slowly began to fall into place.

The events that led up to the accident wound slowly back to the moment she had hurried out from the bar—how long ago? Hours? Or maybe she had lain unconscious for more than what remained of Monday, and it was now Tuesday.

A hollow groan left her lips as she recalled with frightening clarity the argument that had resulted in her walking out. *Storming*, was vastly more apt, she grimaced in retrospect.

'Mrs Andreas?'

Lisa let her eyelids falter open to encounter a white-uniformed nurse bending diligently over her, a hand reaching automatically for her own while the other slid a thermometer between her lips.

'How do you feel?'

'Lousy,' she murmured indistinctly. Her head appeared to be filled with cottonwool, and her voice sounded strange—not hers at all.

The nursing Sister gave a sympathetic smile. 'Doctor will be in to see you soon.'

The extent of her injuries was difficult to determine, and she effected a gingerly visual inspection, breathing a sigh of relief that there was no evidence of anything being broken. Cautiously she wriggled her toes, and winced as pain shot up her leg towards her hip.

'Testing for breakages?'

Lisa looked up, startled, and encountered a pair of blue eyes sparkling with humour. A white coat pronounced his status, and she offered a tentative smile.

'Perhaps you'd care to confirm, or deny—whichever the case may be?'

He didn't hesitate. 'A few nasty grazes, some bruising, mild concussion and shock. X-rays confirm hairline fractures to three ribs, and the left wrist.'

'That's it?'

The grooves deepened each side of his mouth. 'You want more?'

'When do I get out of here?' She asked the question automatically, and blue eyes directed her a twinkling glance.

'Ah, they all say that,' he mused. 'The pretty ones never want to stay.'

A tiny smile curved her generous mouth. 'You're a doctor?'

'With a degree to prove it. Why? Aren't we supposed to be human?'

'Forgive me,' she pleaded faintly. 'You don't fit the image I have of the medical profession.'

'Ah—solemn, dedicated, *distinguished*?'

She met his gaze levelly. 'You haven't answered my question?'

'Which one?'

'How long must I stay here?'

He appeared to contemplate the query, then ventured thoughtfully, 'Your husband is waiting to see you.' His eyes became razor-sharp. 'He's a very influential man.'

Lisa's lids lowered and her fingers plucked at the hem of the sheet. 'I guess this is a private hospital?'

'It is,' the doctor concurred dryly, not adding that Rick Andreas had set up a furore, insisting on summoning the country's best specialists to examine his wife, and to conduct tests and X-rays that were merely routine and well within the capabilities of the hospital's medical staff.

'My injuries are only slight,' Lisa declared pensively, then gave a helpless gesture which incurred a momentary frown.

'I'd like to keep you here for forty-eight hours,' the doctor revealed lightly. 'If I considered the patient warranted further surveillance, I could lengthen that to four days.'

His eyes were far too shrewd, and she forced a slight smile to her lips. 'With a doting husband, a magnificent house complete with servants, it would be ridiculous for me to take up bed-space here.'

'I'll reserve my decision until tomorrow. Okay?'

'Thank you.' She was beginning to feel sleepy, and he moved towards the door.

'Your husband is permitted five minutes,' he declared in parting, then he was gone.

Lisa closed her eyes in a gesture of self-defence as the door opened, and every nerve-end tingled in awareness as she sensed rather than heard Rick enter the room. She wanted to scream out for him to go away, but she didn't possess the strength. Perhaps if she kept very still, he might think she was asleep and quietly leave.

There was no sound, and after seemingly endless seconds she slowly let her lids flicker upwards, encountering the dark inscrutable features of the man standing less than a foot distant.

'How do you feel?'

Lisa fixed her attention on the third button of his immaculate blue shirt. 'I'm assured I'll survive.'

His eyes hardened measurably, then became hooded. 'You could have been killed.'

'I'm not sure whether to be grateful or disappointed,' she murmured without thought, and heard his harsh intake of breath.

'In the name of God—it's hardly a matter for jest!'

Lisa spared him a glance, then wished she hadn't. He looked incredibly angry, and his features were taut and inexorable as he sought to control his temper.

'I'm sure you've already been given all the medical details,' she said wearily. 'Will you please go now? I don't feel inclined to deal with a post-mortem.'

He was silent for an infinitesimal space of time, then he asserted bleakly, 'Sarah despatched a few personal items she thought you might need. I left them with the nurse. Can you think of anything you particularly want?'

She lifted her uninjured hand, then let it fall down on to the counterpane. 'I'm sure Sarah has thought of everything.' For the first time she noticed the regulation hospital garment she was wearing and gave a faint grimace. It was scarcely glamorous attire. The pain began to intensify and she let her head sink back against the pillows. 'I'm tired.' It was true. Besides, she felt fragile and particularly vulnerable. Her lids lowered, the long dark curled lashes heightening her pallor, and she didn't open them even after he had left, making only a slight murmur as the nurse entered the room to elicit a customary check and administer an injection to dull the pain.

When she woke next it was morning, and at first she had difficulty orientating herself with her surroundings. The heavily bandaged wrist felt strange, and ached abominably—in fact, her entire body was one large ache.

Her appetite negligible, she barely picked at her

breakfast tray, and showed little enthusiasm when two nurses appeared at her bedside to urge her into the shower cubicle.

The thought of feeling fresh and clean held some appeal, despite the discomfort any movement caused, and it was heaven to sit on the small plastic stool beneath the portable jet as it cleansed her body. It wasn't until she was standing upright that she noticed the bruising. That several had been incurred by the accident couldn't be disputed, but it was the others—the telltale marks of a lover, that made her writhe with silent embarrassment. How *dared* he? she seethed.

Smelling sweetly of Dior fragrance, and with pillows plumped behind her back, she allowed the nurse to attend to her hair.

'It's so long, and with a natural wave, it's a lovely asset,' the young girl enthused, faintly in awe of her beautiful patient, and the arresting man patiently waiting in the corridor. There were flowers everywhere, and her soft romantic heart was enthralled with it all. 'There,' she murmured in admiration. 'You look so much better. I'll tell your husband he can come in.'

Attired in casually elegant clothes, Rick looked the quintessence of sophisticated success, and his features bore sufficient tender concern to bring a wistful sigh to the nurse's lips as she ushered him in, then carefully closed the door behind her.

'You look very much improved,' Rick told her, moving with indolent ease towards the bed. He lowered his head and brushed his lips against her cheek, then covered her mouth with his own in a brief kiss.

'You've ensured that I receive the best medical attention,' Lisa declared with sombre detachment, then swept her lashes high to meet his gaze. 'Thank you for the flowers,' she murmured with distant politeness. 'They're quite beautiful.'

One eyebrow rose in cynical amusement. 'Still harbouring a grudge, Lisa?'

'Oh, *several*.'

He sat down on the edge of the bed and propped an arm on the other side of her thighs. 'Suppose you tell me.' His eyes were darkly enigmatic, and she wasn't in the least fooled by the slight teasing smile tugging the corners of his sensuous mouth.

'I don't possess the inclination.'

'You're coming home tomorrow.'

Her dismay was clearly evident until she attempted to mask it, and a muscle tensed along his jaw. 'What time?' she asked dully, and was powerless to avoid the hand that reached out to lift her chin.

'Anyone would imagine you were about to re-enter Bluebeard's chamber,' Rick taunted softly. 'Whereas you'll be fussed over and cosseted like a newly-born chick.'

'By Sarah,' Lisa declared. 'And Yannis.'

'But not by your husband?' he mocked. 'Poor Lisa! Is it such a trial being my wife?'

'You know it is,' she threw, sorely tried, and glimpsed his humourless laugh.

'So very bad, hmn, that you would consider risking life and limb to escape me?'

'I was in a rage,' Lisa declared by way of explanation, meeting his level gaze. 'I didn't see where I was going.'

'Do you realise how fortunate you were not to have suffered more serious injury? *Cristos*,' he husked in a harsh undertone, 'have you any conception what I went through when I saw you knocked down by that oncoming car, and powerless to do anything to prevent it?'

'You saw your human asset in danger of liquidation,' she flipped carelessly, and almost cringed at the visible anger evident in those ebony depths.

'Lisa,' he warned emotively, and she shook her head slowly from side to side.

'Go away, Rick,' she said wearily. 'I don't feel I can cope with any recriminations.'

His dark glance speared her mercilessly. 'There are times when you'd try the patience of a saint!'

'Knowing you as I do, I can dispute you resemble any one of those noble disciples!'

He unfolded his length from the bed to tower over her, making her feel at an immediate disadvantage. 'Is there anything you want? Some magazines or books? I'll bring them with me this afternoon.'

'There's no need for such attentive vigilance,' she told him. 'I'm not in any danger.' Not now, not here, she thought silently.

'Nevertheless, I'll call in around two,' Rick drawled, then he turned and moved towards the door. His dark gleaming glance held faint mockery, and she gave into temptation and poked out her tongue in childish retaliation, and could have hit him when he gave a husky laugh.

She couldn't settle after he had gone, and showed little enthusiasm for lunch, despite the fact that it was tastefully assembled and attractively served.

When Rick entered the room a few hours later Lisa was sitting in a chair beneath the window, and she shot him a cursory glance as he deposited a selection of magazines down on to a nearby table.

'Isn't this taking up too much of your valuable time?

Besides, I thought you were supposed to be in Melbourne.' She glimpsed his anger and didn't care. 'Or perhaps you consider it a duty.'

'Duty be damned!' His eyes raked her slightly flushed features and his mouth curved into a wry smile. 'You are my wife, Lisa. Am I not permitted to show some concern for your wellbeing?'

She viewed him circumspectly for all of twenty seconds, then voiced civilly, 'How is Chantal?'

One eyebrow rose in mocking query. 'I wasn't aware we were discussing Chantal.'

'We weren't.'

'But you'd like to, is that it?' he arched cynically, and moving to sit in an adjoining chair he turned slightly to face her. 'What is it that you want to know?'

Now that she had broached the subject, she didn't feel incumbent to pursue it further. After all, how could she demand, 'What does she mean to you? Were you lovers—are you still?' Such a query would be tantamount to an admission of sorts, and that would never do. He might begin to think she cared, and she didn't. He could wine and dine any number of women and it wouldn't matter a jot.

Aloud, she began, 'She's a—fascinating woman. Have you known her very long?'

'A few years,' Rick informed her, his features assuming mocking cynicism. 'Could it be that you're jealous?'

'Of course not,' she responded swiftly, fixing her gaze somewhere beyond his shoulder.

'How do you feel?'

Lisa contemplated the query, then said slowly, 'Do you really want to know?'

He seemed to take an age to answer, and his voice was

dangerously soft. 'You should thank God for your injuries. Otherwise I'd take you severely to task for daring to question my motives.'

There was no doubt he meant every word, and she suppressed an involuntary shiver. He wasn't a man to suffer fools gladly, and she wondered at her own temerity in attempting to anger him.

'Are you in any pain?'

She shifted her gaze and met his penetrating dark eyes. 'It's bearable,' she conceded evenly. 'My ribs hurt, so does my wrist, and my body feels like it's been used as a punching bag. Otherwise I'm fine.'

'There's much bruising?'

'Yes,' she reiterated fiercely, all her latent anger coming to the fore. 'But then I already had several bruises beforehand. No thanks to you!'

His eyes gleamed in sudden comprehension. 'Ah, I see,' he murmured. 'You're angry that those love-marks have been witnessed by others, eh?' A faint smile twisted his lips. 'Did it bother you very much?'

'Yes!' she hissed, mortified by his amusement. 'I hated it!'

His teeth gleamed white. 'Never mind. I shall have to make it up to you.'

'You'll do nothing of the kind!'

'I have an appointment at three,' he mused, standing to his feet, then he bent forward and brushed his lips across her forehead. 'I'll see you tonight.'

'Such solicitous regard isn't necessary,' she declared waspishly. 'I'm coming home tomorrow. I'll see you then.'

'And have me thought an inconsiderate, unattentive husband? Sarah and Yannis—not to mention the nursing staff—would never forgive me,' he mocked lightly.

'Well, I don't want you to come,' she cried, then winced as pain shot down her side. Perhaps it was delayed shock, or anger, but her eyes filled with tears, and with an impatient gesture Rick moved towards the door.

'I'll get the doctor.'

'Oh, for heaven's sake!' Lisa protested. 'I'm all right.'

Rick spared her a long thoughtful look. 'I will have him check you, just the same.'

When he had gone, she sat in contemplative silence, then after a while she stood to her feet and crossed to switch on the television, viewing the small screen with pretended interest until the nurse brought in the dinner tray, and afterwards she leafed through the magazines Rick had brought until the doctor put in an appearance.

At ten past seven she glanced at her watch, then continued reading. Ingrid and James arrived, and were suitably solicitous, bearing fruit and a new novel currently heading the bestseller list.

When they left Lisa stood to her feet, removed her dressing-gown, and slid into bed. A strange bereft feeling that Rick wasn't coming after all depressed her, and at nine when the nurse came to settle her down to sleep, she could barely summon a smile.

In the darkness she felt unaccountably cross with herself. After all, she'd told him not to come. Why should she miss his presence? Yet she did, and a few silent tears of self-pity slowly wended their way down her cheeks to rest at the edge of her chin before rolling down her throat. It was crazy! Images danced before her eyes, and she could see his features clearly. The strong profile, the broadly etched bone structure, dark ebony eyes that could gleam with humour or become bleak with chilling anger. A wide sensuous mouth that could tease and taunt with little provocation, and wreak havoc with her senses. She almost ached with longing just to touch him, and have him touch her. Remembering how he had made love was pure folly, and with a tiny groan she turned her head into the pillow and wept.

CHAPTER EIGHT

RICK appeared shortly after two the following afternoon, dwarfing the room and causing the nurses to flutter coyly in his presence. Lisa attempted to be objective about it, assuring herself she didn't give a *darn* if they found him attractive or not. Yet if she was truthful, her own heartbeat quickened when he brushed his lips against her temple in an outward gesture of affection. Her reaction made her cross, for she was still harbouring a grudge over his high-handed behaviour regarding her supposed clandestine meeting with Tony.

'You didn't come last night.' The accusation was there, and Rick cast her a speculative glance.

'If you remember, you were rather adamant that I should not.'

'I thought you would take any chance to play the attentive husband.'

'You must be feeling better,' he decided, vaguely amused, and Lisa subsided into resentful silence. After all, it was difficult to be indignant when sitting in a wheelchair with a nurse in attendance.

Showing solicitous concern, Rick saw her safely seated in the car, then crossed round to slip in behind the wheel. This was the moment she had been dreading, for now the recriminations would start, and she didn't have the energy to parry the inevitable barrage of questions.

However, Rick was surprisingly silent, and didn't venture so much as a word during the ten-minute drive to Vaucluse, and upon bringing the car to a halt outside the entrance of his—*their* home, she corrected, the door opened to reveal Yannis and an anxious Sarah, and within seconds she was engulfed in a series of greetings and enquiries about her health.

'I think you should rest,' Rick declared, viewing her pale features with a faintly narrowed gaze, and she swept him a telling glance.

'That's all I've been doing for the past few days.' She moved towards the lounge, uncaring whether he followed or not. 'I'd like some coffee, and one of Sarah's scones.'

'After which you'll go upstairs to bed.'

'In the middle of the afternoon? Don't start ordering me about like a child,' she warned, and sensed his impatience.

'By the grace of God—you never learn!'

Lisa sank into a nearby chair with a drawn-out sigh. 'Oh, for heaven's sake! Do we have to argue? I've only just stepped in the door.'

He lifted a hand and raked it through his hair, ruffling it into attractive disorder. 'There are times when I find it difficult not to *shake* you!'

'Please don't,' she quipped with a rueful grimace. 'I'm really rather fragile at the moment.'

She suffered his long penetrating stare with a calm she was far from feeling. It wasn't fair that he could arouse such a gamut of emotions—from desire to hate to downright antipathy. 'Oh, go away, Rick,' she murmured wearily. 'I don't feel up to arguing with you, and if you stay in this room much longer, we undoubtedly *will*.'

'I'll be in the study,' he imparted brusquely. 'Sarah will undoubtedly put in an appearance the minute I leave.' Crossing to the door, he opened it and then quietly pulled it shut behind him.

Lisa slumped back in the chair, feeling totally enervated. Perhaps she was weaker than she thought, for she was sure if she closed her eyes she could slip into sweet oblivion of somnolence. Rick was an overpowering entity at the best of times, and right now she didn't possess the strength of a kitten.

Sarah pushed open the door bare minutes later, then quietly retreated to summon her employer, who, on glimpsing the waxen-pale features in repose, bent low and gently lifted her into his arms and carried her upstairs, shaking head in refusal of his housekeeper's offer to help.

In the bedroom, he crossed and lowered her down on to the bed, then slipped off her shoes, adjusted the pillow, and spread a blanket over her recumbent form. Then he took a nearby chair and shifted his length into it, adopting a vigil he had no intention of abandoning.

Lisa was dreaming, reliving again the nightmare of those blaring lights, the sudden screech of brakes, and *felt* the thud of impact, and she screamed, coming awake in an instant and unable to relate her surroundings with the seeming reality of what she'd just left behind her.

'It's all right,' a male voice soothed. 'You're home. Just relax.'

His face came into line with her vision and she began to cry, not great gulping sobs, but stupid little hiccups that hurt abominably.

Rick sat down on the edge of the bed and leant forward, brushing his fingers across her forehead as he tucked back a stray lock of hair behind her ear. 'Do you want something to drink?'

She shook her head, and in an unbidden gesture she edged her tongue out to the corner of her mouth and caught the single tear that had rolled to rest there. 'How long have I been asleep?'

His smile was oddly gentle. 'Four hours. Are you hungry?'

Was she? She couldn't really concentrate on anything with him so close.

'I think we'll get you into bed, hmn? Then I'll send Sarah up with something light to tempt your appetite.' With ease he lifted her to stand before him, then began undoing the buttons of her dress.

'I can manage,' she said shakily, and glimpsed his slight cynicism.

'With one hand? Just stand still,' he bade, unbuckling the belt at her waist with sure fingers. Within minutes she was divested of all her clothes, and when he reached for the clip on her bra she made a protesting murmur which went unheeded.

Reticence was responsible for the hands that crept up to her shoulders, crossing over her breasts in an oddly defensive gesture.

'So shy?'

'I don't see you in the role of nursemaid,' she choked as he reached for her nightgown.

'Lift your arms.'

'I can manage,' she declared stoically.

'You're beginning to sound like a record caught in a groove,' Rick slanted musingly. 'Be a good girl and do as you're told, hmn?' His gaze narrowed slightly as she began to comply, and she met his eyes with a shade of defiance.

'They're only just beginning to fade.' Her voice

choked with hidden anger. 'Oh, the nurses were very diplomatic—not one passed comment.' Brown eyes flashed with bitterness. 'But I knew that they knew what caused these marks, and I hated it!'

'Poor Lisa,' Rick mocked softly. 'Such an innocent! Do you think you're the only female ever to bear the bruises of a man's passion?'

'Lust!' she threw wildly. 'How can you call it anything else?'

He leant forward and let his fingers brush down her cheek to rest at her chin, tilting it up so that she had to look at him.

A strange warmth began to course through her veins, and with an inaudible groan she twisted her head. 'Don't!'

'Don't—what?'

'Please—I couldn't bear it,' she begged, and her eyes widened into huge pools as he lowered his head.

As his mouth closed over hers she gave a convulsive sob, but his lips traced her own with incredible gentleness, exploring, cajoling—something he had never done before. It had a melting effect, rendering her weak-limbed and malleable, and she shuddered as he trailed his lips down to the gentle swell of her breasts. Slowly, and with infinite tenderness, he caressed each bruise in turn, and she agonised as his mough began an evocative trail over each sensitive pulse-beat until she felt every nerve-end come alive with tingling warmth. Then his mouth moved up to cover her own, savouring the sweetness that was hers to give, until with an odd reluctance he gently pushed her to arms' length.

'Let's get that nightgown on, shall we?' His eyes gleamed with wry humour as she looked down at her faintly flushed features. 'In your present state of health, I refuse to be tempted.'

'I wasn't trying to tempt you!'

A slight smile twisted his lips. 'Not consciously, perhaps,' he allowed lazily. 'However, your body has a will of its own.'

It was true, but there was no way she would admit to it! Aloud, she said with deliberate sweetness, 'If you've quite finished playing nursemaid, I'll get into bed.'

Rick's faint chuckle was almost her undoing, but she managed to control the urge to retaliate. Perhaps she was in a weakened state, after all!

Sarah arrived with an attractively laid out tray, and a deep red rosebud reposing in a delicate crystal vase for decoration. Considering roses were out of season, Lisa was touched by the housekeeper's thoughtfulness.

'There's soup, and a nice omelette,' the older woman declared, sparing Lisa a sympathetic smile. 'I thought something light, that you could manage without any help. And there's a small bowl of fresh fruit salad to follow.'

'Thanks, Sarah, you're an angel.' She gave a self-effacing grin. 'I'm being outrageously spoilt!'

'You gave us all a nasty shock. Mr Andreas insisted on staying overnight at the hospital, and rarely stepped outside its doors until yesterday. He's been very worried about you—we all have.'

Lisa glanced up, then quickly let her lashes lower to disguise her surprise. 'I was hurrying to cross the road and didn't see a thing until it was too late,' she attempted to explain, dismissing it lightly.

'It could have been a tragedy. Praise be you escaped serious injury,' Sarah declared fervently.

'Oh, I'm made of tough stuff, Sarah,' Lisa assured her jokingly. 'In a few days I'll be like new again.'

'It's to be hoped so. Mr Andreas has been quite distraught.'

Has he, indeed? Lisa mused. It would jolly well serve him right!

The meal was delicious, and she finished every morsel, so that when Rick entered the room nearly an hour later he glanced first at the empty tray, then at her. 'Sarah will be pleased,' he drawled, and she pulled a face at him.

'I feel like a seven-year-old child confined to the sickroom. All that's missing is a pile of toys with which to amuse myself.'

His eyes twinkled with devilish humour. 'Will a bed-time story suffice instead?'

'Little Red Riding Hood?' she broached without conscious thought. 'With you assuming the role of the Wolf?'

'Is that how you see me?'

He had moved to stand beside the bed, and she watched in mesmerised fascination as he removed the tray on to the pedestal, then lowered his length to sit on the edge of the bed.

Exuding sheer animal magnetism, he possessed the power to stir her senses, bringing an awareness she found vaguely shocking. The thought crossed her mind that if they had met under different circumstances she would have found it impossible to resist him. As it was, she continually fought against an increasing attraction, refusing to accept that he had been motivated by anything other than analytical ruthlessness in marrying her. It didn't augur well for the relationship, yet she was helpless to discover any solution.

'What's going on inside that head of yours?'

The light mocking query disrupting her thoughts, and she blinked at the sensuality evident. Her eyes seemed drawn to his mouth, and she could almost *feel* its touch upon her own. What was worse—she wanted for him to kiss her. Not the deep wounding possession that bruised, but she ached for his gentleness, some indication that he might actually care.

'I've been waiting for you to pounce,' she managed lightly, and saw his eyes narrow speculatively.

'Ah, I see,' he drawled. 'Your—ex-boy-friend. Tony, I believe?'

Lisa released a deep sigh, then winced as her ribs protested with a shaft of pain. 'I didn't arrange to meet him. It was purely by chance that we even saw each other. He asked me to have a drink with him to show there were no hard feelings, and I accepted.' Her dark-fringed lashes swept slowly upwards without any pretence to guile. 'I saw no reason why I shouldn't.'

He viewed her thoughtfully. 'We've been married only a matter of days. To see you in the company of any man, much less someone who had meant something to you, was unacceptable.'

She began to feel angry, and thrust him a vexed look. 'Yet if the tables were reversed, and I entered a bar or restaurant and saw you sitting with another woman, you'd wonder what all the fuss was about if I behaved as you did.'

'Perhaps.'

'Oh, balderdash! Any man would!'

His faint smile only succeeded in making her even

more angry. 'So, am I to understand this particular diatribe is not aimed solely at me?'

'Yes—*no*, damn you!'

'Let's call a truce, shall we?' He withdrew something from the pocket of his jacket and tossed a small jeweller's box into her lap.'

'What's this?' Lisa looked at it as if it contained something of devious origin.

'Open it and see,' Rick bade easily, and rather shakily she snapped open the catch.

A magnificent diamond teardrop pendant sent myriad colours bursting from its many facets. She couldn't help but admire its brilliance, nor could she restrain a tiny gasp of pleasure. 'For me?' Her eyes swept up to meet his. 'But why?'

He didn't answer at once, reaching out to lift the delicate chain from its velvet bed and fasten the tiny clasp beneath the heavy swathe of hair at her nape.

The diamond nestled warmly in the delicate valley between her breasts, and she gave a slight smile. 'It looks out of place with a nightgown.'

'I agree,' he drawled. 'I far prefer you wearing no clothes at all.'

'Thank you!'

One eyebrow slanted with mocking cynicism. 'For daring to suggest I find you desirable?'

Lisa swallowed convulsively. 'The pendant.'

'So—thank me.'

'Perhaps I shouldn't,' she declared ruminatively. 'There's a proverb to do with a Greek bearing gifts.'

'Are you afraid I might demand something in return?'

'You not only demand, you take without askance,' Lisa declared shakily.

His features became an enigmatic mask, and she watched as he rose to his feet.

'Is there anything else you want before you settle down for the night? Sarah is bringing you a hot drink.'

Slowly she shook her head, and without a further word Rick turned and left the room.

Hours later she was still awake, sleep proving an elusive captive as she wrestled with her conscience. She wasn't in any pain, thanks to the tablets she had taken earlier, but a strange restlessness besieged her, making it impossible to settle.

At last, unable to bear it any longer, she slid from the bed and gingerly slid on a wrap. Then without further thought she moved from the room into the hallway and made for the stairs. A few lamps had been left on, providing sufficient illumination, and she made her way down to the lower floor.

As she reached the study door she restrained a mirthless laugh. What if he was out? Then her mission would be all in vain.

Taking a steadying breath, she placed her hand on the knob and stepped into the room to be confronted by a blaze of light.

'What in the name of *hell* are you doing here?'

Savage anger emanated from every pore, and she almost turned and ran. Only stoic determination and a measure of courage stilled her flight.

There was nothing else for it but to begin. 'It's not my birthday, and nowhere near Christmas,' she struggled valiantly. The fingers of her right hand lifted to touch the pendant, and she met his gaze fearlessly.

Dark eyes narrowed as he leaned back in his chair, and it took all her resolve to remain where she was. In this sort of mood, he was diabolical—a dark angel, and if she wasn't careful, he'd unleash his temper upon her hapless head.

'I'm—sorry if I offended you by being somewhat—facetious.'

He regarded her thoughtfully, and took his time before speaking. 'You came all the way downstairs at this time of night to tell me that?'

'I couldn't sleep,' she said simply, and the corners of his mouth twisted to form a wry smile.

'It's almost midnight.'

'I'm sorry if I disturbed you,' Lisa ventured politely.

'You sound like a well-mannered schoolgirl,' Rick mused. 'Come here.'

Her eyes widened, and she felt her pulse begin an erratic beat. 'I think I'll go back to bed.' If she didn't, she'd probably regret it!

'Lisa.'

His voice was a deep drawl, and she moved slowly towards the large executive desk as if drawn by some will other than her own.

She came to a halt within touching distance, unable to move a further inch. 'It's awfully late for you to be working,' she said distantly. A strange magic was beginning to weave its spell, mesmerising her into a state of complete disorientation.

'Because of the International Dateline, there are some calls that have to be put through at this witching hour,' Rick drawled, and he leant back in his chair to survey her carefully assembled features, then said softly, 'I shan't bite you.'

'I'm not sure I should believe you,' she ventured shakily, and he smiled, startling her with its warmth, and her eyes widened with fascination.

'You wanted to thank me?' he prompted lazily, his dark gleaming eyes sliding slowly to the pendant, then back to her lips.

'Thank you,' she began dutifully. 'I'll take good care of it.'

The corners of his eyes creased with amusement. 'Oh, come, surely you can do better than that?'

Her teeth began to worry the lower edge of her lip, then she leaned forward on impulse and planted a fleeting kiss near the edge of his mouth.

'Only one?' he mocked. 'Surely such an expensive bauble deserves something more?'

Lisa tried desperately to maintain her composure, but her eyes gave her away. Slowly she lowered her head, and the instant her lips brushed his, firm hands caught hold of her waist, steadying her, and she grasped his shoulders for support. She had never kissed a man like this, taking the initiative. Rick let her do the exploring, becoming responsive as she would have drawn back.

'Please!' It was a plaintive murmur that went unheeded as he lifted her on to his lap, and she became lost as the blood pulsed through her veins. A slow warmth began deep into the pit of her stomach and spread to encompass her whole body, and she gave a low moan as his hand moved aside the lacy bodice. Her arousal was all too evident, and she glimpsed the slumbering passion in his eyes as he gently disentangled her arm.

'It's time you went back to bed.' His smile was warm, and with one fluid movement he stood to his feet with her in his arms.

She felt infinitely secure, and it was a feeling she never wanted to lose. As if in a dream, she watched him turn off the lights, then mount the stairs, and in their room he placed her gently down on to the bed.

He gave her a long, faintly brooding look, then crossed to the bathroom. When he came back, she was filled with a lambent trembling warmth, and each separate nerve-end came tinglingly alive as he slipped in beside her. She kept her gaze lowered, and saw him reach out for the lamp, then the room was plunged into darkness.

The following few days passed uneventfully. Days during which she rested at Rick's express instruction, aided and abetted by Sarah, which, while being wholly admirable, tended to lend itself to boredom. After all, she wasn't *sick*, she assured Sarah on more than one occasion. Her injuries had been superficial, and her wrist was no longer painful—merely providing a twinge now and again if she exerted any pressure or attempted unthinkingly to twist it. However, Sarah merely shook her head, insisting that shock was known to have nasty repercussions, and blandly continued to treat her charge as an invalid. Rick was his usual indomitable self, proving immune to each and every plea she made to be permitted outside the gates, until she railed at him in fury that he was intent on keeping her a *prisoner*.

'Not at all,' he drawled, shooting her a dark indolent glance across the breakfast table. 'A friend of mine is down from the Gold Coast on business, and we'll dine with him this evening.'

'Here?' Lisa asked, hoping he'd elect an alternative venue.

'No. I have made a reservation at an exclusive establishment in Double Bay.'

'For three?'

'For three,' Rick concurred sardonically, draining the last of his coffee. He uncurled his length from the chair and moved with indolent ease towards the door. 'Be ready at six.' Then in a single stride he moved out of sight, and she drew a deep pleasurable sigh.

Already her mind was whirling with what she would wear, and by late afternoon she felt alive with anticipation. She couldn't remember being so pleased at the thought of dining out. The fact that she was due to be in the company of her formidable husband, and, in all probability, his equally formidable friend, didn't matter at all!

She took incredible care with her appearance, choosing a glamorous pantsuit in white silk. Small pleats at the waistband belled out in elegant folds at the hips, then tapered down over the calves of her legs. The top was sleeveless, and the neckline, back and front, was deeply scooped with several folds forming a cowled effect. With it she wore delicate high-heeled gold sandals, and added gold accessories in the form of a chain at her neck and wrist. Make-up was kept to a minimum, except for her eyes, which she highlighted with shadow and mascara. A touch of blusher added colour to her cheeks, and she used a deep red on her lips.

'Hmn, very nice,' Rick drawled as he entered the bedroom, and his dark gleam of admiration did strange things to her equilibrium.

'Thank you.' She was supremely conscious of him, almost as if each part of her was honed to a fine pitch in awareness of his presence. It was crazy to feel like this about a man she actively disliked. But you don't dislike him, a tiny voice taunted.

'I'll go downstairs while you shower and change,' she said evenly, endeavouring not to blush beneath his mocking gaze.

'Afraid to stay?'

'Not at all.' If only he knew how much courage it took for her to stand there calmly when every defence mechanism urged her to run—*fast*. 'However, I feel like a drink.' She managed a seemingly careless shrug and moved towards the door.

'I'll join you in about fifteen minutes.'

She didn't bother to answer, and took the stairs down to the lower floor, crossing to the lounge where she made for the bar and mixed herself a generous brandy, lime and soda with ice.

'Looking forward to the evening?'

Lisa turned slightly, her eyes remarkably clear as she met his cynical smile. The Ferrari purred along the New South Head Road with an almost silent smoothness, and in an effort to steer the conversation away from anything that might endanger their present truce, she asked idly,

'Tell me something about your friend. If he's a close associate, it will probably seem strange if I know nothing about him.'

Her ploy didn't fool him at all, and he slanted a quizzical glance before revealing with musing cynicism,

'Ryan is a highly successful realtor based on the Gold Coast. We went to the same university, and enjoy a few joint business investments. As for expecting you to be aware of his existence,' he drawled, 'he knows we're newly married, and will imagine we have other things on our mind.'

Lisa refused to be drawn, and she made no demur

when Rick took hold of her elbow as they entered the restaurant.

'Mr Marshall is at the bar, Mr Andreas,' the *maître d'hôtel* informed him courteously. 'Do you wish to join him, or shall I send a message for him to make his way to your table?'

'The table, I think,' Rick essayed. 'Perhaps you could send over the wine steward?'

Ryan Marshall was the epitome of male sophistication. He bore a faintly cynical, almost jaded air, and there was a hard implacability in his manner that was all too familiar.

'Good of you to join me,' Ryan intimated smoothly, casting Lisa a devastating smile. 'So this is the girl who managed to persuade Rick into the enviable state of matrimony!' He lifted his glass with a shade of mockery. 'May it be a long and happy union.'

'You'll have to forgive his cynicism,' Rick drawled. 'Shall we order?'

'Good idea,' the other man concurred. 'I had to skip lunch.'

Rick turned towards Lisa. 'May I make a suggestion, or will you consider it an infringement on what you consider your feminine freedom of choice?'

She tilted her head slightly. 'Suggest, by all means,' she slanted solemnly.

'The salmon mousse as a starter, with lobster thermidor. Agreed?'

'I'd prefer pawns, with a side salad.'

Ryan began to chuckle. 'There speaks a woman who knows her own mind! You'd get on well with my wife,' he drawled, and Lisa successfully hid her surprise.

'I didn't realise you were married.'

'Estranged,' he corrected dryly, and Rick intervened smoothly,

'Let's reach a decision, shall we? The waiter is waiting our order.'

The salmon mousse was delectable, and Lisa had just forked the first morsel of prawn into her mouth when a soft feminine voice intruded.

'Rick—Ryan! What a lucky guess!'

Lisa kept her expression deliberately bland as she finished her mouthful, then summoning a polite smile she turned and proffered with seeming sweetness, 'Chantal. Nice to see you again.'

'Daddy said you were in town, and I guessed you'd both dine out,' Chantal trilled vivaciously. 'We're such old friends, I thought I'd join you.' Her eyes turned towards Rick and she almost devoured him. 'You didn't return my call, you naughty man.'

'Sit down, Chantal,' Ryan drawled. 'You're creating a disturbance.'

Lisa thought it was nothing like the disturbance *she'd* like to create!

'Well, Lisa can't be expected to have two gorgeous men all to herself,' Chantal pouted provocatively as she slid into the chair opposite. 'It simply isn't fair!' Her eyes took in Lisa's appearance at a glance, then narrowed as she caught the elasticised wrist support. 'Good heavens, darling, isn't that more suited to the tennis court? Or is it some new fashion accessory?'

'Lisa was recently involved in a car accident,' Rick explained, and the Greek girl gave a negative shrug.

'I'm fine, thank you,' Lisa declared with a sarcasm that missed its target entirely.

'No injuries?' Ryan slanted, and Rick told him,

'None to speak of—fortunately.'

'Such a shame,' Chantal proferred with obvious lack of interest, and Lisa's faint smile was a mere facsimile.

'Yes, wasn't it?'

It was hardly a propitious evening, and she became increasingly incensed as Chantal continued to monopolise the conversation to a point where Lisa was ignored almost completely.

At ten she pleaded a headache and asked to be taken home, offering to summon a taxi if the others wanted to remain. Both men rose to the occasion, despite Chantal's protestations, and Ryan called for the bill.

'I shall see you again,' he murmured as they left the foyer and made their way out onto the street. 'Rick is a lucky man.'

'Perhaps you'd care to dine with us through the week?' Lisa asked politely, and he shook his head.

'Not this time round, I'm afraid. I fly back to the Coast tomorrow.'

She made a suitable rejoinder, then felt Rick's steely grasp on her elbow as he bade them goodnight.

'You appeared to get on well with Ryan.'

Lisa cast him a quick glance, then swung her attention back to the swiftly passing street lights. It had turned cold, and she suppressed a slight shiver. 'Shouldn't I?' she queried lightly. 'He reminds me of you,' she added ruminatively, and heard his faint laugh.

'Indeed?'

'I imagine his wife found him equally impossible to get on with,' she brooded, and his response brought a faint blush to her cheeks.

'I take it that's meant to be a condemnation?'

'Chantal, of course, finds you both totally irresistible.'

'My, my! I felt sure her name would creep into the conversation sooner or later.'

Her teeth clenched tightly together as she attempted to keep a rein on her temper. 'If you don't mind, I'd rather not discuss it. I have a headache, I'm tired, and I want to go to bed.'

'So you shall,' he drawled, easing the car into the driveway. 'Tomorrow, you'll rest.'

'Tomorrow,' she declared waspishly, 'I shall do precisely what I like!'

In the bedroom she undressed and slipped into bed, then plumped the pillow vigorously and turned on her side at the furthest side of the bed.

Rick's faint chuckle only served to infuriate her further, and she stoically ignored him, lying rigid as he slid in beside her.

In the darkness he reached for her, stilling her protests with ease, and in the end it was she who clung to him with an urgency that afterwards made her writhe with shame.

'I'll be home late,' Rick told her as he was about to leave the following morning. 'Don't wait dinner for me.'

'Oh!' Her disappointment was a tangible thing, despite the fact she tried to hide it, and he slanted musingly,

'Just—"oh"? No questions as to my whereabouts, or why?'

She effected a slight shrug. 'What difference does it make?'

'None whatsoever,' he dismissed hardily, then he was gone.

Damn! She hadn't meant to sound so trite. The words had just slipped out, and now she couldn't retract them.

The day stretched out in front of her with little or no seeming importance, and with a muffled exclamation she crossed to the phone.

'Ingrid? Care for some company this afternoon?'

'Why, *Lisa*! How are you?'

'I thought I'd come and see the children, have a coffee and a chat with you. Would two o'clock be all right?'

'Oh, Lisa, I'm most terribly sorry. I'd really like to say yes, but I have an appointment I simply can't postpone, and Simon has to attend a school recital practice.' Ingrid sounded quite contrite. 'Can we make it tomorrow?'

What else could she say? 'Tomorrow will be fine.'

Who else could she ring at this hour of the day? Dammit, she had to talk to someone, do *something*, or she'd go mad!

'Roberto? It's Lisa. How is the world of fashion these days?' she queried lightly, and heard his answering chuckle.

'Considering you only left it some ten days ago, I can hardly be expected to provide anything new!'

'Nothing interesting?'

'What's the matter, my sweet? Don't tell me you're missing the catwalk and the camera?'

'Actually, I thought I might call into the studio,' she declared idly. 'Or is there a show on somewhere?'

'Tonight, and we're one model short. Susie is out of action, nursing a sprained ankle.'

Lisa clutched the receiver. 'Let me do it. I'd love to, honestly.'

'Well,' he deliberated, 'it certainly would solve our problem. Check with your husband, and call me back.'

'Oh, he won't mind,' Lisa declared with blithe disregard. 'Tell me where and when, and I'll be there.'

It wasn't until she was actually backstage, waiting to be called, that she began to have second thoughts. Rick, if he found out, would be furious. Yet how could he? she assured rationally. The show finished at ten, and she'd be home fifteen minutes later. Before that, if she could slip away early. In any case, if was too late now.

The venue for the show was a prestigious inner city hotel renowned for its select clientèle, and the auditorium was filled to capacity. The show had been co-ordinated so that a different bracket of clothes was shown between courses, giving the patrons the opportunity to enjoy their food.

It wasn't until halfway through the evening that Lisa glimpsed a familiar dark head, and her attention became riveted as she met Rick's narrowed, deliberately enigmatic gaze.

How she managed to smile and continue as if nothing had happened, she never knew, for inside she was a shaking mass of pitiful nerves. As soon as she had completed modelling the last of the range, she stripped and literally threw on her own clothes before escaping out the side door.

'Going somewhere?'

Lisa came to an abrupt halt. 'I suppose you want an explanation?' She hardly dared look at him. As it was, she could almost *feel* his anger.

'You don't think I deserve one?' Rick queried sardonically, and she drew a deep calming breath.

'Is this an inquisition? Can't we discuss it at home?'

'Be assured we shall,' he drawled hatefully. 'I assume you drove here?' At her faint nod, he took hold of her arm. 'I'll have the concierge place my car under security for the night. We'll use yours.'

Lisa didn't utter so much as a word during the length of time it took to reach Vaucluse, and once indoors she made straight for the stairs, uncaring whether he followed or not.

In the bedroom she crossed to her bathroom suite, stripped and stepped beneath the shower, then emerged to slip on a thin silky wrap before re-entering the bedroom.

Her steps slowed and came to a halt as she saw Rick's tall frame standing near the window. He turned and she almost died at the inimical anger evident.

There was nothing for it but to begin. Anything else was madness. 'I rang Ingrid,' she said slowly. 'She couldn't meet me for lunch, and had other plans for the afternoon.' Her gaze was remarkably steady. 'Roberto mentioned that he was one model short for tonight, and I suggested I fill in. Is there anything drastically wrong with that?'

'You are my wife,' Rick declared implacably, and she burst into angry speech.

'Does that preclude me from *everything*?'

'I see no necessity for you to put your body on full view for every salacious male to covet.'

'My God! Anyone would think you possess sole licence to it!'

His eyes darkened measurably. 'But I do,' he stressed cynically. 'We made a bargain, Lisa,' he reminded her hardily. 'Any transgression, and I'll wring your slender neck!'

'Oh, go to hell, Rick!' she threw, uncaring of any retribution. 'I can't bear overly-possessive men!'

'Then you'll be relieved to enjoy a temporary respite,' he taunted. 'I have to catch the early flight to Adelaide.

Four days, Lisa. Dare I suggest you might miss me?'

'Not a hope,' she flung tautly. 'Now, if you've finished I'd like to go to bed.'

'There speaks the voice of wisdom,' he mocked. 'Retreat is infinitely advisable under the circumstances.'

She didn't say another word, although she inwardly seethed, and despite a feeling of exhaustion, sleep was an elusive captive until almost dawn, and when she woke it was to discover that Rick had left more than two hours previously.

CHAPTER NINE

LISA lay back in the chair, feeling infinitely relaxed as the beautician administered a facial treatment. A girl sat on a stool near her feet, giving her a pedicure. An hour before, she had visited the hairdresser.

With a small sigh, she closed her eyes, lulled by the latent anticipatory warmth that sang through her veins at the mere thought of seeing Rick again.

Four days—the same number of *nights*. Dear heaven, she ached with a strange longing that made her restless and discontent in the need for fulfilment. He had become part of her, and his absence had given her time in which to think—to become aware that her feelings were involved to a degree where she couldn't envisage life without him.

She had planned dinner down to the finest detail, enlisting Sarah in a conspiracy that saw the preparation of his favourite dishes. The formal dining-room would be set for two, with the silver candelabrum and an exquisite floral arrangement as a centrepiece. The best damask, silver and bone china would adorn the table, accompanied by a cherished set of crystal goblets. It would be a meal to remember, and afterwards—well, there was little doubt what form *afterwards* would take!

'You look beautiful, Mrs Andreas.'

Lisa gave the beautician a singularly sweet smile. 'Thank you.' There was no conceit in her manner, and she paid the fee without the slightest qualm.

162

She felt fantastic, and it showed in her dark gleaming eyes, the lightness of her step as she made her way through the arcade to the busy city street.

It was almost five, and she paused on the pavement as she waited for the traffic lights to change so that she could cross to the adjacent car park. There was a news-stand nearby, and she took out her purse, extracting the necessary coins, then caught the late edition beneath her arm and hurried as the pedestrians began to surge across the road.

Negotiating peak-hour traffic took all her concentra-tion, and it was with a sense of relief that she turned the Mazda into the driveway some thirty minutes later and brought it to a halt outside the main entrance.

Yannis opened the door, his smile widening into an expansive beam of admiration as she entered the foyer.

'Mr Andreas is in the lounge.'

She stopped mid-step, her eyes widening with a mix-ture of consternation and delight. 'He's here? Now?' A hand went automatically to her hair, smoothing its length in a purely nervous gesture. 'I didn't think he was due in until six.'

'I believe he caught an earlier plane,' Yannis revealed with a wide grin as he caught her swiftly changing expression.

Now that Rick was actually here, her courage de-serted her, and she fought down a desire to run upstairs. Let him come after her, instead of the other way round. Then common sense prevailed, and she crossed the parqueted floor to the wide panelled doors, waiting patiently as Yannis opened them before entering the lounge, and she felt her stomach give a sickening lurch as the door clicked softly shut behind her.

Her eyes swept hungrily to the man standing indolently at ease a few feet away from the magnificent marble fireplace. He held a glass in his hand, and he swirled the contents idly as he watched her move slowly towards him.

She faltered to a stop halfway across the room, and she pushed her hands behind her back lest he glimpse evidence of her nervousness.

'Hello,' Lisa greeted him quietly. 'How was your trip?'

His dark eyes gleamed with mocking cynicism and his lips gave a sardonic twist as he let his gaze wander at will over her slender curves. 'Hello yourself,' he murmured lazily. 'Don't I merit a little more enthusiasm?'

The edge of her tongue edged out and ran its tip over the fullness of her lower lip. 'I think I'd like a drink.'

'You shall have one—after you've bestowed a wifely welcome,' he concluded with a tinge of amusement.

'I don't really think I can,' she said shakily. 'You might suddenly swoop.'

An eyebrow lifted. 'Now why should I do that?'

She caught the edge of her lip with her teeth, then proffered hesitantly, 'We didn't exactly part on the best of terms.'

'Neither we did,' Rick drawled. 'However, I'm inclined to be of the opinion that arguments are an integral part of our life.' His eyes took on a devilish gleam. 'Now, are you going to kiss me, or do I have to come to you?'

A slow impish smile curved her generous mouth. 'Perhaps we could meet halfway?'

His husky laugh was her undoing, and she flew into his outstretched arms, revelling in the deep indolent passion evident in his eyes the instant before his mouth closed over hers in a possession that left her in no doubt of his arousal.

'Hmn,' he drawled a long time later, 'I suppose Sarah has spent the entire day planning dinner. We shouldn't disappoint her.'

Lisa stood in the curve of his arm, her whole body alive with a wealth of tingling sensation. 'Definitely not,' she reproved teasingly. 'Now can I have that drink?'

'Minx!' he scolded with a tigerish growl. 'I'm not at all in the mood for drink—or food.'

She slanted him a dancing glance. 'You'll just have to suffer. It would be positively indecent to retire before nine—at the earliest.'

'Remind me to exact due punishment,' he threatened mockingly, and she laughed.

'I'm sure you will,' she declared quizzically. 'but it will be your punishment as well.'

Rick's kiss was hard and forceful, but she didn't object to his strength, and at last he put her at arms' length.

'When does this epicurean feast begin?'

Lisa spared a quick glance at her watch. 'Six-thirty. We expected you to arrive at six, and allowed thirty minutes for you to shower and change, then have a drink.'

There was a discreet tap on the door, and at Rick's voiced command Yannis entered wearing a look of abject apology.

'I'm terribly sorry.' His eyes swept to his employer. 'Mr Marshall is calling long distance. He says it's important.'

Rick stifled a muttered expletive, then murmured an apology. 'I'll take it in the study.' He dropped a brief hard kiss down on to her lips, then strode from the room.

Lisa stood bemused, a slow sweet smile curving her mouth.

'The newspaper, Mrs Andreas,' Yannis interceded. 'Shall I remove it?'

She turned to face him. 'Oh no, thank you.' She held out her hand. 'I'll glance through it while I'm waiting.'

Seated in a nearby chair, she opened the front page and idly scanned the headlines, then leafed a few pages, read her horoscope, turned to the comic-strip section, and was about to place it on to a nearby table when a photograph caught her eye.

There was a caption above it, and the usual descriptive blurb beneath. But it was the two people pictured that riveted her attention. If she was in any doubt, the print clarified it.

'Mr Rick Andreas, international broker and corporate director, in Adelaide on business, dining at Regine's with Miss Chantal Roussos'.

Lisa's hands began to shake so much she had to put the newspaper down. She felt her head pound, and an icy band seemed to clutch hold of her heart and squeeze until she experienced physical pain. She wanted to cry, but no tears would come, and with a calmness that amazed her she stood to her feet, folded the newspaper and walked from the room, crossing the foyer to the stairs, and in her bedroom she moved to the bed and slipped the paper beneath her pillow. Then she retraced her steps down to the lounge.

Rick was standing in almost the same position as he had been when she had first entered the lounge. How long ago—ten, fifteen minutes? It seemed like hours.

'Sarah has just told me dinner can be brought forward,' he said. 'Shall we go through to the dining-room?'

She seethed, inwardly hating him. But he would never have guessed it, for her smile was warm with just the right degree of humour as she took his outstretched hand.

As an actress, she was superb. A veritable Sarah Bernhardt, in fact. From the starter, through the main course, to the completion of dessert, she put on an exemplary performance. She raised her glass to his, smiled and met his dark gleaming gaze with seeming provocative guile. She even surpassed her own expectations.

Electing to forgo coffee, she stifled a slight yawn. 'I think I'll have an early night.' She cast him a slanting glance. 'You must be tired after going to so many business meetings, and all those other trivialities.'

'I trust that's an invitation,' Rick drawled, and she let her lips widen into a bewitching smile.

'Why, darling, what do you think?' Standing to her feet, she moved across the room, and managed to flinch as his arm curved round her waist as they reached the stairs.

In their bedroom she crossed straight to her bathroom and changed into a nightgown with admirable speed, then moved to the bed, quickly extracted the newspaper and spread it out over his pillow at the appropriate page.

She only just completed the deed when he emerged from his bathroom. Trying to view the man objectively, he looked infinitely *male*. There was a careless, carefree air about him, his hair ruffled and the deep-grooved, vaguely devilish smile almost succeeded in demolishing her defences. Almost.

Lisa watched as he crossed to the bed, waiting as he caught sight of the newspaper, then his look sharpened as he directed a narrowed glance across the width of the bed.

'The free licence of the journalistic press,' he commented significantly. 'They take one-tenth fact and embellish it with nine-tenths fiction.'

Her gaze was remarkably level. 'You don't deny you took Chantal to dinner?'

He lifted a hand and raked it through his hair. 'I didn't take her anywhere. Her father was in Adelaide. He attended the same meetings.' He gave an indolent shrug. 'Chantal came along for the ride.'

'Oh, I'm sure she wouldn't miss an opportunity to accompany Daddy,' Lisa declared mockingly. 'Especially when she knew you'd be there.'

His eyes narrowed fractionally. 'What the photo doesn't show,' he drawled, 'is that there were four other people present at the table. We left together, but that was all.'

'I see.'

'Do you?' Rick arched. 'I have the feeling you've already drawn your own conclusions.'

'Can you blame me?' she cried, sorely tried.

'What do you want? A minute-by minute account of my every move?'

'I don't want anything,' she blurted, hating him for attempting to turn the tables by applying logic to something she considered totally illogical.

'All right, Lisa,' he declared hardily. 'What now? Do we digress into another slanging match?' His features became an iron mask. 'For the space of a few hours I thought you'd actually missed me.'

'You should be so fortunate!'

With an angry movement he caught up the newspaper, bunched it into a ball and threw it to the farthest corner of the room. 'So help me, I could shake you until every bone in your body rattles!'

He looked angry enough to do just that, and she turned away. 'I'm going to bed. With something like five bedrooms available, any one other than this will suffice.'

'The hell you will,' Rick declared harshly. 'You will sleep here, in this bed, with me. Even if I have to tie you there!'

'Try it!' she threw rashly, rounding on him with fury, and almost died at the harshness of his expression.

Without a word he crossed towards her, moving with swift ease as she attempted to evade him.

Hard hands caught hold of her arms, and she gasped as he lifted her towards the bed. She struggled, her strength an impotent apology against his as he pinned her to the mattress, and she gave a despairing moan as his mouth closed over hers in a brutal savage possession.

Minutes later he rolled on to his side, his eyes sharpening as they took in her swollen lips. 'Go to sleep, Lisa,' he bade mockingly, and she clenched her hands against the fresh tide of anger.

'I could kill you!'

'I lie in fear and trembling,' Rick drawled, adding silkily, 'Another word, and I'll bring my hand into painful contact with your delicately-rounded rear! Something,' he added wryly, 'I should have done a long time ago.'

'You despicable fiend! Dare, and I'll—'

She never finished the threat, and instead issued a

startled yelp as he swept down the covers and administered a hurtful, demoralising spanking.

Pride ensured she didn't utter a single cry, and afterwards she rolled on to her stomach and buried her head beneath the pillow, hating him afresh for making her suffer such an indignity.

Lisa woke in the morning to the sound of the shower in the adjoining bathroom, and the events of the previous evening came flooding back to taunt her. This time yesterday she had been eager for the new day, and what the evening would bring. Now, it was as if her world lay in pieces at her feet.

A slight sound alerted her attention, and she glanced up to see Rick standing at the foot of the bed.

'Get up,' he instructed tersely. 'We're leaving for the airport in an hour.'

'I'm not going anywhere,' she insisted hollowly.

'You are,' he declared with invincible clarity. 'Even if I have to dress you myself, and carry you.'

'Charming,' she sneered bitterly. 'Why the sudden rush?'

'Accept that it suits me.'

Her eyes sparked alive. 'Well, it doesn't suit *me*!'

'Too bad,' Rick asserted bluntly, and Lisa bunched the pillow and eased herself into a sitting position.

'What is this? Another example of male chauvinistic mastery?'

His look was startlingly direct, his jaw taut as he surveyed her. 'Just do as you're told, Lisa,' he threatened. 'Otherwise, so help me, I'll do something regrettable.'

'You mean—*more?*' she threw deliberately, letting

her eyes rake his tall frame from head to foot and back again. 'I thought you'd subjected me to every indignity imaginable.'

Without a word he crossed to the bed and tore the covers off, then as she scrambled to the other side of the bed he reached out and caught her, lifting her with ease to stand struggling wildly before him.

'Do I dress you—or will you do it yourself?' he queried silkily, and she wasn't in any doubt he meant every word. There was a hard diabolical anger beneath the surface of his control, and only a fool would tempt him further.

'I'll do it,' she capitulated, sweeping him a vengeful glare. 'If you'll let me know how long we'll be away, I'll pack accordingly.'

'Two, three days. All you'll need is a swimsuit and a change of clothes.'

'Where are we going?'

'Does it matter?'

'Tell Sarah I'll be down for breakfast in half an hour,' Lisa declared wearily, and with a hard glance he released her and left the room.

Yannis drove them to the airport, and with the minimum of formality they boarded the commercial jet bound for Coolangatta in south-east Queensland.

Rick was uncommunicative, and that suited Lisa, for she didn't feel inclined to keep up a patter of small-talk.

Upon touch-down Rick collected their overnight bags from the luggage-bay and she followed him to a waiting Land Rover which, much to her surprise, transported them to the far end of the tarmac and a waiting helicopter.

'Where on earth are we going?'

'You'll see when we get there,' he taunted, and she had little choice but to let him assist her into the cockpit.

'Ever ridden in one of these whirlybirds before?'

Lisa looked at the pilot and spared him a smile. 'Yes. More than a year ago.' It had been on a modelling assignment to an unaccessible spot in the far north, and the last leg of the journey had been completed in an identical machine.

'Okay, you know what to expect,' he grinned, and reached for his headphones. 'Must say I envy you, being able to get away from it all.'

'What does he mean?' Lisa asked, turning towards Rick, but the noise from the engine and blade rotation forbade a reply.

They flew out to sea, then followed the coastline north. Surfer's Paradise from the air was an awesome sight, rather like she imagined Hawaii would look, on a smaller scale. The sea was a deep translucent blue with foamy-crested surf rolling to the foreshore. Golden sand provided an apron for the numerous apartment buildings that towered high in varying architectural design.

Within ten minutes the helicopter began to descend, and Lisa peered through the perspex dome to ascertain their destination. A small dot of an island lay to the east, and as they drew nearer it grew larger, covered for the most part with dense green foliage.

A helipad on the foreshore provided a setting-down point, and Lisa eased herself out of her seat and suffered Rick's hands at her waist as he lifted her down.

'Thanks, Bruce. I'll radio you when we want to be picked up.' He caught the overnight bags that were tossed down, then Lisa was led along the pontoon-bridge.

As they reached the sand, the helicopter lifted off the pad, and with a wave the pilot urged it out over the ocean and back, presumably, from where they had come.

'What now?'

Rick turned briefly and gave her a cynical smile. 'We go up to the house.'

Surprise was clearly evident on her expressive features. 'What house? I didn't see anything from the air.'

'You weren't meant to,' he responded dryly. 'This is my own private retreat. No phones, only radio control for any emergency.'

'You own it?' she asked with incredulity, and glimpsed his wry smile.

'Yes.'

She was struggling to keep up with him, his long strides far outpacing hers. The path they were following wasn't much more than a track, but within seconds they came to a clearing, and as he moved aside she gave a gasp of disbelief.

A stucco residence lay like a jewel amongst its surroundings. White, with slatted shutters, it resembled something out of another world. Suddenly she knew what it reminded her of—photos she had seen in a pictorial book on Greece. By design, it was a replica of those tiled, stuccoed villas that graced the hillsides of endless harbours throughout the mainland and islands of Greece.

'It's beautiful,' she said simply.

'Let's go indoors.'

She followed him up the short flight of steps, then through the thick-panelled door into the tiled foyer. Like a child embarking on a fascinating discovery she moved from room to room, noting the spartan but functional furnishings. Built around an inner courtyard, in which there reposed a sparkling pool, the villa was square in design, with large airy rooms opening into the courtyard. There were three bedrooms, each with en suite facilities, a large lounge, dining-room, a room equally large for entertainment, as well as a well-equipped kitchen and utility room.

It was like an oasis in the middle of the desert of modern civilisation, and she turned back to face him with a slow smile. 'How can you bear not to live here?'

One eyebrow lifted sardonically. 'The pressures of corporate directorships forbids it.'

'Do you come here often?'

'Whenever I feel the need to get away from it all, and business permits,' he shrugged indolently.

'And now it does?'

'No,' he responded cynically, and she cast him a puzzled glance.

'Then why did we come?'

His look was startlingly direct. 'Because I want to attempt to set back the clock.'

Lisa's stomach gave a sudden lurch. 'What do you mean?'

His twisted smile held an edge of humour. 'I'm going for a swim. Do you want to join me?'

A faint frown momentarily creased her brow, then she gave a slight shrug. 'I'll go and change.'

'There's no one to see whether you're suitably clothed,' Rick mocked, and she swung startled eyes up to meet his.

'Are you suggesting I swim naked?'

'Why not?' he queried carelessly, his eyes agleam with devilish mockery, and she voiced without thought,

'Are you?'

'Unless it offends you.' One eybrow slanted in silent query, and she was momentarily at a loss for words.

'I-it's your island, your pool,' she said in slightly strangled tones, and caught his amusement the instant before he turned towards the large sliding doors leading out on to the courtyard.

Lisa tried to tell herself she'd call his bluff, but when it came to divesting her clothes she found she couldn't ignore her inhibitions, and quickly slipped into bikini briefs and tied the straps of the minuscule top. Grabbing up a towel, she wrapped it sarong-wise around her, and tucked in the edge, then she slid open the door and moved to the side of the pool.

Rick's dark head was visible at the far end, and she watched as he surfaced several metres from where she stood.

'Come on in,' he bade, silently mocking her, and with indolent grace she lifted her hair and tied it into a careless knot atop her head, then undid the towel and let it fall to the ground.

His husky laugh brought an answering grin, and she dived neatly into the pool.

'You didn't quite possess sufficient courage, hmn?' he teased, and she scooped a handful of water into his mocking face.

'You didn't expect me to cast convention aside, surely?'

A rakish gleam entered his eyes. 'There's an easy remedy to that,' he declared purposely, moving close with a single lithe stroke, and the laughter died as he reached for the ties at her nape.

'Don't,' she murmured shakily, her eyes widening as

she become shockingly aware of him. 'Please!'

'Are you pleading with me?'

His teasing humour was an unknown entity, and she was unsure how to deal with it. Isolated as they were, there was no Sarah or Yannis to whom she could appeal, and she was suddenly aware of her vulnerability.

His fingers were light as they caressed the hollows at the edge of her throat, and she let out a tiny gasp as they trailed down over the swelling curve of her breast.

He was standing on the tiled floor of the pool, the water lapping gently around his midriff, and she attempted to move back, only to have him curve a hand round the back of her waist holding her still.

'Hmn,' he murmured lazily. 'I'm almost inclined to take what was denied me last night.' His eyes were faintly hooded and dark with passion.

'You can't be serious,' she said shakily.

'About making love to you?' he mocked gently.

A latent warmth seemed to move like quicksilver through her veins, and her body seemed to sway of its own volition towards him.

'I was never more serious.' His voice was a deep lazy drawl, and as he caught the gamut of emotions chasing across her expressive features its timbre changed subtly. 'But if I attempt it now, *here*, it will undoubtedly prove an affront to your modesty,' he concluded with a trace of wryness.

'You're not usually so—considerate.' Rick's eyes narrowed and she hurried on, 'We've only been married a matter of weeks,' she offered tentatively, wrestling with the need to find the right words. 'Under circumstances that could hardly be termed advantageous.' Her lashes swept upwards as she searched those etched darkly tanned features for some visible sign that would give her the courage to continue. 'There are legal documents stating that I must stay with you for five years.' She couldn't hold his gaze, and her eyes slid to a point beyond his left ear. 'I thought I could do it, but I can't—not any more.'

'Care to tell me why?'

The water had suddenly lost its warmth, and she shivered. How could she tell him she'd fallen desperately in love with him? It would make her position as his wife intolerable. At least if she pretended to hate him, he would never discover the depth of her feelings. To even contemplate him knowing was enough to make her afraid. For then he would have her completely in his power. At least this way she could retain a modicum of self-esteem.

'Isn't it time for lunch?'

'Oh, Lisa,' he berated gently, shaking his head. 'What am I to do with you, hmn?' His mouth lowered to cover hers, teasing, coaxing, until she opened her lips like a flower to the sun, uncaring that they might divulge her secret as passion superseded transitory warmth.

Somehow they were out of the pool, and she stood bemused as Rick gently towelled her dry, then removed the excess moisture from his skin. With a low exultant growl he lifted her into his arms and carried her into the bedroom.

Her eyes searched his, unconsciously begging him to ease the deep throbbing ache within, but his hands began a slow tactile exploration, seeking and finding hidden hollows. The delicate curves of her breast swelled at his touch, the nipples hardening as they began to pulsate, and she gave a low moan as he took first one and then the other between his teeth to render an erotic sensual ecstasy.

Not content, his mouth trailed at will over her body, alternatively teasing and demanding until she could stand it no longer.

'Rick—please! Don't,' she groaned, and she twisted her head from side to side in an effort to free herself of the havoc he was causing.

Still he refused to desist, and she cried out at the exquisite pain, reaching for his head and dragging it away. 'Oh God—no more, *please!*' she sobbed quietly, and her whole body shook as he effected an unerring possession that took her to the heights and beyond.

CHAPTER TEN

WHAT remained of the day took on a dreamlike quality. They swam, played like children in the shallows of the sparkling sea, took a long leisurely walk around the island, then after raiding a well-stocked deep freeze, Lisa thawed a pre-cooked meal, heated and served it with chilled wine, hot crunchy bread rolls, and made a fresh fruit salad with fruit picked from the trees lining the foot of the garden.

'Being here is like living in another world,' she mused as she handed Rick his coffee.

Rick patted the seat beside him. 'Come and sit down.' His eyes held a latent warmth she couldn't ignore, and her breathing began to quicken as she sank down on to the sofa.

Idly he reached out and picked up a swathe of her hair, letting it run through his fingers as if it held an immeasurable fascination.

'I-it's too long,' she murmured indistinctly. There was something almost pagan in his dark brooding look, and she was unable to still her rapid pulse-beat or stop the faint tinge of pink that crept into her cheeks. Suddenly she wished she smoked, for it would give her something to do with her hands. Polite conversation had never seemed more difficult to summon, and in an attempt to cover her nervous agitation she said stiltedly, 'I forgot to bring the brandy. You usually have some with your coffee.'

'Don't ever have it cut.'

Surprise made her look at him, and his lips curved into a slow smile. 'Your hair is beautiful, like a living mantle of velvet silk.' He lifted a handful of it to his lips and brushed them against its length. 'So fresh and clean. I love to see you unadorned, with this flowing over your shoulders.' His voice was frankly sensuous, and she shied away like a frightened colt as he trailed his fingers down her cheek. 'Shy, Lisa?'

'Please—don't,' she pleaded almost desperately, and heard this soft chuckle.

'Don't—what? Make love to you?'

Helplessly she searched for something to distract his attention. 'Your coffee is getting cold,' she ventured, trying to move away without success.

'To hell with coffee,' Rick murmured, bending his head down to hers.

Lisa felt his lips at her temple, and they slid to caress an earlobe before seeking the sensitive hollow at the base of her throat. A slow lethargy seemed to take possession of her limbs, rendering them boneless, and she couldn't have moved away if she tried. When his mouth closed over hers she made a slight movement in protest, but a hand slid up to her nape, holding her head fast, while another at the small of her back propelled her close to the hard length of his powerful frame.

Lisa felt as if she was slowly drowning, lost in a world of sensuality that melted her very bones. Never in her wildest imagination had she thought to experience such a maelstrom of feeling.

Rick stood to his feet and lifted her into his arms. In the bedroom he slowly divested her of every vestige of clothing, then began on his own.

Gently he pulled her unresistingly towards him, and his mouth descended to begin a kiss of such incredible tenderness she thought she would die from the very feel of it. Of their own volition her lips parted, and she felt his faint intake of breath, then his mouth hardened with bruising possession as she met and matched his ardour with total abandon.

When she woke the sun was filtering through the slatted shutters, making a slanted pattern across the tiled floor and part of the wall.

'Come on, sleepyhead,' a deep voice drawled. 'If you stay there much longer, I'll be tempted to join you.'

Lisa glanced towards the door and saw Rick leaning lazily against its aperture. He was wearing faded blue levi's, and had a short-sleeved cotton shirt tucked into the waistband.

'What time is it?'

'Almost ten,' he told her dryly. 'I've already made breakfast.'

She shot him a startled glance, and a wicked smile curved her lips. '*You* have? My goodness, maybe there's hope for you yet.'

He shrugged himself away from the door and took a few ominous steps towards the bed. 'What do you mean by that remark?' The grooves that ran down each cheek deepened. 'Implying that your husband is incompetent, eh?'

A light impish laugh bubbled to the surface. 'Only in the kitchen,' she elaborated quizzically, and he gave a deep throaty laugh, his eyes frankly sensuous as they began a slow appraisal of her sleep-tossed hair, the faint glow of her skin above the covering sheet.

'Is that an admission?'

'I refuse to tell you,' she declared sedately. 'On the grounds that it might inflate your already outsize ego.'

There was hidden laughter in his eyes as he bent down and bestowed a leisurely kiss, then he lifted his head to regard her bemusement with gleaming mockery.

'I'll get up,' she said half-heartedly, and heard his chuckle.

'Do you really want to?'

'I think so. I'm hungry,' she offered, slipping aside the sheet. 'Give me five minutes to have a shower.'

'We could, of course, dispense with breakfast and have an early lunch,' he slanted, and she laughed.

'In this instance, food is high on my list of preferences.'

'I'll let you get away with it this time,' he mocked, making a play to grab her, but she managed to evade him and ran to the adjoining bathroom.

Ten minutes later she was sitting at the kitchen table eating fresh fruit, and washing it down with a glass of iced water.

'What are we going to do today?' Lisa voiced the query idly, not at all concerned, as long as they spent it together.

'I have a small boat,' Rick informed her. 'We could try to catch a few fish for dinner.'

They did precisely that, and to her delight, it was she who hooked the first and only fish.

'Talk about role reversal,' she grinned mischievously, handing him the line. 'I thought the male of the species was supposed to be the hunter.'

'There are many ways to hunt,' he teased, his dark eyes gleaming with humour, and she poked her tongue out at him.

'I hereby donate you my fish.' Her nose wrinkled expressively. 'I caught it—you can clean it.'

'We've been round the island, having anchored in three different spots,' Rick ruminated, sparing a glance at his watch. 'I doubt we'll catch any more. Shall we go back?'

'Whatever you say,' Lisa declared meekly, and laughed as he raised a mock threatening fist. 'You're just sore you didn't prove your superiority,' she laughed, eyeing their solitary catch.

The remainder of the day went quickly, and after an evening meal which they both helped prepare they strolled down on to the beach.

'We're about to embark on our second moonlight stroll,' Rick began idly, bending down to pick up a pebble and skim it along the sea's surface.

'That seems a long time ago,' Lisa mused, glancing out towards the horizon, then she turned to him. 'Do you realise I know very little about you?'

He cast her a slanted musing glance. 'Ask away.'

'Tell me about your childhood,' she said slowly. 'Where you were born, where you grew up. Parents, sisters, brothers—family,' she ended simply.

'Why the sudden need to know about my roots?' he queried with a trace of cynicism, and she slid her arm through his, wanting to be close to him.

'You know all there is about me,' she said slowly, looking up to ascertain his mood, and unable to determine much in the dim half-light.

'I was born in Athens, the eldest son of wealthy parents. I have two sisters, both married, and both living within a few kilometres of each other. At the last count, I'm uncle to three nephews.'

A slight frown creased her forehead. 'They live in Athens?'

'My parents, yes.' His voice was deliberately enigmatic. 'They emigrated to Australia when I was fifteen, but after two years they longed for their native Greece and returned, taking my two sisters. They were too young to express an opinion.'

'I see,' Lisa said quietly, and met his dark glance.

'Do you?'

'You must have been torn between the two,' she voiced softly. 'Your family, or a fresh start in a new land.'

'It wasn't an easy choice,' he revealed expressionlessly.

'And your sisters?'

'They grew up and married eminent Greek men,' he mocked lightly.

'Do you ever visit them?'

'Often,' he said dryly. 'I return every year.'

'I'm glad,' she said simply.

'Did you imagine I was an outcast?'

'Most European men and women are very family-conscious. I couldn't imagine you being an exception.'

They walked on, enjoying a mutual silence, until Lisa turned towards him, voicing the thoughts that had been bothering her over the past thirty hours.

'Why did we come here?' She stumbled over the words in an attempt to elaborate. 'I mean—why *now*?' A flashback of conversation suddenly came to her mind, tempting the query, 'You mentioned something about wanting to turn back the clock.' She turned slightly to face him, searching in the dim light for some visible expression, but it proved elusive.

'I'm an impatient man,' Rick revealed slowly. 'I need to clarify a situation that otherwise might take more time than I care to contemplate.'

A sudden pain in the depths of her stomach made her almost cry out. Dear God! Did he mean their marriage? Had she been such a disappointment to him? Anguish robbed her voice. Why should she imagine he might love her? *Love?* She stifled a bitter laugh. She was just an object, someone with whom he could slake his physical lust. Three weeks they had been married, and now he wanted out. A hollow feeling entered her heart. He employed the best legal brains in the country, and she entertained no doubt he could dispense with those documents as easily as he had coerced her to sign them. In fact, she wondered if they weren't some elaborate sham.

'I'm going back to the house,' she managed shakily, and fled before he had a chance to stop her.

'Lisa!'

She heard him calling, but she didn't pause, and she reached the clearing when hard hands reached out and caught hold of her.

'Why the hell did you run away?'

'Leave me alone!' She wrenched her arm out of his grasp and took two further steps before he brought her to a halt. 'Let me go, you—*fiend*!' she gasped emotively.

'Let's go inside, shall we?'

Rick's voice was like ice, but she didn't care any more.

'Inside, outside—what does it matter?' Her eyes blazed with brilliant fire. 'These—past few days have been an attempt to let me down gently, I suppose? Who is it, Rick? Chantal?'

When he didn't answer she turned and flailed her fists against his chest, hitting him wherever she could, uncaring that he made no attempt to fend off her blows.

'Answer me, damn you!'

'Why are you so angry?'

His soft drawl was the living end, and without thought her hand flew to his face, and in the still evening air the slap sounded incredibly sharp.

'Because I hate you,' she snapped furiously. '*Hate* you, do you understand?'

'Indeed? Is that why you're moved to such fury at the thought of a possible—er—dissolution of our marriage?'

Angry spent tears flowed over and slowly rolled down to rest at her chin. 'I want to go back to Sydney,' she managed resolutely. 'As soon as it can be arranged.'

'So we shall,' he told her imperturbably. 'But not for a few more days.'

Lisa stared up at him wildly. 'But I can't stay here that long!'

'Why?' Rick demanded quietly. 'Are you so afraid?'

When she didn't answer, he drawled,

'Not of me—yourself.'

Was she that transparent? It would be the final humiliation if he discovered her feelings. She'd rather die than be an object for his amusement!

'It's no use,' she declared shakily. 'We seem to drive each other to violence with practically no provocation at all.' She looked up at him, feeling strangely disorientated. She was still suffering from shock and anger. Never in her life had she resorted to hitting a man—or anyone, for that matter. As long as she could remember she had possessed the sunniest of natures, her disposition pleasant, and she was considered to be kind-hearted by family and friends. Why should this devilish man have the power to turn her upside down—bring forth a latent rage that was totally alien to her character?

'Lisa.'

When she didn't look at him, he reached out and tilted her chin. 'You stubborn, argumentative little *fool*!' he growled huskily. 'What do I have to do to convince you?'

Her eyes widened into huge brown pools of incredulity, and she stood still, hardly daring to breathe.

'I was aware of your existence,' Rick extolled quietly. 'I made it my business to be informed of everything relating to your brother's interests. His personal life, family, associates.' A wry smile momentarily twisted his lips. 'A large amount of money was required to bail out his company in order to put it back on its feet. Sentiment simply does not enter a prospective business arrangement. My informant compiled a thorough dossier, and I was intrigued. I'd reached an age where I considered the stability of marriage to be an asset, yet most—in fact, all,' he went on dryly, 'my feminine companions were more interested in my money and social standing, than the man himself.' His fingers tightened fractionally, then slid down to cup her throat. 'By the grace of God—or fate, I was given the opportunity to kill both birds with one stone, as the adage goes.'

He paused, his expression becoming deliberately inscrutable, and his thumbs moved absently back and forth over the throbbing pulse at each side of her throat, creating havoc with her equilibrium. 'The first time you saw me—at the fashion show, during the afternoon of the evening we were formally introduced by your brother,' he reminded her ruminatively. 'I had, as you accused, come to "inspect the merchandise", and dinner that evening merely served to endorse my intention. It

was simply a matter of presenting James with an ultimatum. In the present economic climate, there was no one
else from whom he could raise the necessary finance,
and I was aware that the bond between you was very
strong.' He took time to marshall his thoughts, deliberately taking care to utilise the correct words as he
continued, 'You intrigued me from the beginning. So
cool, but underneath, a fiery little termagant. In my
arms you became a warm and infinitely passionate
woman, and if I had cold-heartedly precipitated our
marriage, the accident proved just how much you had
come to mean to me.' His eyes darkened measurably.
'*Cristos!*' he husked softly, 'have you any conception of
what I went through? Seeing you run, and powerless to
reach you in time? I suffered the tortures of the damned
for days! The hours immediately following the accident
were sheer hell while the medics determined your injuries, and then I wasn't content, insisting that eminent
consultants be summoned to ensure your condition
wasn't more serious than I'd been informed.' His head
lowered and his lips brushed hers, then traced the
delicate bone-structure of her face. 'How could I tell you
with words that I loved you? It was too soon, and
besides, you were battling with your own emotions,
swinging between hate and passion with predictable
regularity.'

A slow glimmer of hope began to shine through the
mists of her misunderstanding. 'Chantal—'

'Was never in the running,' he declared hardily, own-
ing ruefully, 'I can't deny I've known many women—I
would hardly be human if I pretended otherwise. But
none I've felt impelled to marry.' He gave a self-derisory
laugh. 'It's never been a necessity.'

'No,' said Lisa in a small voice, 'I don't suppose it has.'

A slight shake brought her head up to look at him, and he caught the utter desolation evident for an instant, then with a muttered oath he pulled her close.

'I love you,' he husked gently. '*You*, the heart and soul that has little to do with the way you look.' His eyes darkened and became slumbrous with passionate intensity. 'I could live to a hundred, and never tire of being with you—*loving* you.' His mouth covered hers in a kiss that succeeded in removing every last vestige of doubt, and when he lifted his head she stood starry-eyed and breathless, a shaft of exquisite longing beginning to unfurl deep inside her.

She wanted to cry and laugh at the same time, and she looked up at those dark, arrestingly powerful features with a sense of wonderment, amazed that she could ever have actually hated him. Slowly she lifted a hand to his face, and her fingers shook as they touched the hard muscle and bone at the edge of his jaw. 'I hit you.'

His eyes gleamed with devilish amusement. 'Indeed you did. Quite hard, for a slender slip of femininity!'

'I'm sorry,' Lisa whispered, feeling incredibly ashamed, and glimpsed his widening smile.

'I shall see that you make some form of atonement,' Rick murmured teasingly, and her lips parted, then curved into a winsome smile.

'Oh?' She let her eyes widen with deliberate guile. 'When is this—er—atonement to begin?'

'Very soon,' he drawled, pulling her close against the hard length of him.

Instinctively she pulled his head down to within touching distance of her own and placed a fleeting kiss against the edge of that sensuously moulded mouth. 'I love you,' she said simply.

A long sigh left his lips an instant before they trailed down to bury themselves against the sensitive throbbing pulse at the base of her throat, then he moved his mouth slowly up to possess the sweet softness that was his alone.

It was a long time before he lifted his head, and he took in her softly parted lips, the deep passion darkening her eyes.

'I'd begun to despair that I would ever hear you say those words.' His lips brushed hers, then lifted with obvious reluctance. 'You're in my blood, like a wild sweet wine. I can never let you go.'

Gently Lisa disentangled his arms, then caught hold of his hand. 'Shall we go inside?' she suggested quizzically, wrinkling her nose at him as he began to laugh.

'Is that an invitation?'

A soft bubble of mirth rose to the surface. 'Do you need one?'

'I *ache* with the need to make you part of me,' Rick assured her with a tigerish growl, and a tide of tumultuous longing swept through her veins.

'Then what are we waiting for?' she husked provocatively, exulting in the strength of the arms that swept her high as he carried her indoors.

Take 4
Exciting Books
Absolutely
FREE

Love, romance, intrigue... all are captured for you by
Mills & Boon's top-selling authors. By becoming a
regular reader of Mills & Boon's Romances you can
enjoy 6 superb new titles every month plus a whole
range of special benefits: your very own personal
membership card, a free monthly newsletter packed
with recipes, competitions, exclusive book offers and
a monthly guide to the stars, plus extra bargain offers
and big cash savings.

**AND an Introductory FREE GIFT for YOU.
Turn over the page for details.**

As a special introduction we will send you four exciting Mills & Boon Romances Free and without obligation when you complete and return this coupon.

At the same time we will reserve a subscription to Mills & Boon Reader Service for you. Every month, you will receive 6 of the very latest novels by leading Romantic Fiction authors, delivered direct to your door. You don't pay extra for delivery — postage and packing is always completely Free. There is no obligation or commitment — you can cancel your subscription at any time.

You have nothing to lose and a whole world of romance to gain.

Just fill in and post the coupon today to **MILLS & BOON READER SERVICE, FREEPOST, P.O. BOX 236, CROYDON, SURREY CR9 9EL.**

Please Note:- READERS IN SOUTH AFRICA write to Mills & Boon, Postbag X3010, Randburg 2125, S. Africa.

FREE BOOKS CERTIFICATE

To: Mills & Boon Reader Service, FREEPOST, P.O. Box 236, Croydon, Surrey CR9 9EL.

Please send me, free and without obligation, four Mills & Boon Romances, and reserve a Reader Service Subscription for me. If I decide to subscribe I shall, from the beginning of the month following my free parcel of books, receive six new books each month for £6.60, post and packing free. If I decide not to subscribe, I shall write to you within 10 days The free books are mine to keep in any case. I understand that I may cancel my subscription at any time simply by writing to you. I am over 18 years of age.

Please write in BLOCK CAPITALS.

Signature _____

Name _____

Address _____

_____ Post code _____

SEND NO MONEY — TAKE NO RISKS.

Please don't forget to include your Postcode.

Remember, postcodes speed delivery. Offer applies in UK only and is not valid to present subscribers. Mills & Boon reserve the right to exercise discretion in granting membership. If price changes are necessary you will be notified.

EP86

6R   *Offer expires December 31st 1984*